THE DEGENERATES

THE DEGENERATES

New York London Toronto Sydney New Delhi

$\mathcal{A}$
atheneum

J. ALBERT MANN

An imprint of Simon & Schuster Children's Publishing Division
1230 Avenue of the Americas, New York, New York 10020

Text copyright © 2020 by J. Albert Mann
Jacket illustration copyright © 2020 by Sarah Maxwell
For information about special discounts for bulk purchases, please contact Simon & Schuster Special Sales at 1-866-506-1949 or business@simonandschuster.com.
The Simon & Schuster Speakers Bureau can bring authors to your live event. For more information or to book an event, contact the Simon & Schuster Speakers Bureau at 1-866-248-3049 or visit our website at www.simonspeakers.com.
Book design by Rebecca Syracuse
The text for this book was set in Belizio.
Manufactured in the United States of America
First Edition
10 9 8 7 6 5 4 3 2 1
Library of Congress Cataloging-in-Publication Data
Names: Mann, Jennifer Ann, author.
Title: The degenerates / J. Albert Mann.
Description: First edition. | New York City : Atheneum Books for Young Readers, [2020] | Includes bibliographical references. | Audience: Ages 14 Up. | Audience: Grades 10-12. | Summary: In 1928, Maxine, Rose, Alice, and London face vicious attendants and bullying older girls at the Massachusetts School for the Feeble-Minded, each determined to change her fate at all costs. Includes historical notes about eugenics.
Identifiers: LCCN 2019035673 | ISBN 9781534419353 (hardcover) | ISBN 9781534419377 (eBook)
Subjects: CYAC: Inmates of institutions—Fiction. | People with disabilities—Fiction. | People with mental disabilities—Fiction. | Friendship—Fiction. | Bullying—Fiction. | African Americans—Fiction.
Classification: LCC PZ7.M31433 Deg 2020 | DDC [Fic]—dc23
LC record available at https://lccn.loc.gov/2019035673

To every girl who has ever been
told to *take it down a notch.*

—J. A. M.

THE DEGENERATES

London couldn't stop thinking about the girl in the iron lung. The metal barrel had been keeping the girl alive now for two weeks. It was the same amount of time that London realized she had been keeping something alive inside her. One had nothing to do with the other, London knew, but she couldn't help connecting them. Three miles away a girl was encased in a machine that was pushing air into and pulling air out of her lungs, tethering her to life. Just thinking about it made London suck in a deep breath of chilly October air as she walked down Chelsea, knowing that this air was sinking deep inside her . . . tethering her to a life, a very small life.

Better to think about the machine.

She pictured a bellows-like tool shoving air into each of the girl's lungs, which London imagined looked like the pigs' bladders hanging out to dry at Flannery's butcher shop on Decatur.

The iron lung fascinated her. Not the polio part.

London knew sickness well enough. Sickness had taken both her parents, along with thousands of others, ten years before, when the flu had swept through Boston. The only memory she had of her parents was the morning they'd all docked at the commonwealth pier following the long trip over from Abruzzo. It had been the summer of 1918, and she'd been only four years old, but she remembered her mother's nervous, excited eyes as the ship pulled alongside the largest building London had ever seen. She remembered her father swinging her onto his shoulders, the smell of his hair, the feel of his smile through the long reach of her arms around his chin. He was dead within a month. Her mother didn't last much longer. Sickness whisked people away from you in an instant—it was what it was. Girls living day in and day out inside iron machines, that was something else.

London felt close to the girl somehow. She herself had spent many nights trapped inside filthy orphanage dormitories or in even filthier foster homes, sleeping in rooms full of people she didn't know while some sort of bellows-like force kept her alive.

Two weeks ago—the day the girl went into the iron lung—London had vomited into the leaf-choked gutter on her way to school. After spitting out as much as possible of the nasty taste of the old lady's watery oatmeal and wiping the thick spit from her face with the back of her hand, she had turned toward the butcher shop on Decatur Street, and then stood on the sidewalk until Alby came out.

It had only taken him a moment to understand. London had always admired this about Alby, how quick-witted he was—his mind whipping colorfully about like the long row of flags lining the front of the Fairmont Copley Plaza on St. James. Her own mind moved more at the speed of the old milk wagons along Meridian. Although the expression on Alby's face that morning was anything but colorful. Instead it had matched the bleached-out apron he wore, too early in the morning to be splashed with the dark red of blood. When he didn't move from the shop door, London understood.

Alby was done with her.

She'd approached him. Controlled. Except for her eyes, which she could feel burning in their sockets. Alby didn't move—as quick as his brain worked, it wasn't quicker than London's boot, and she kicked him hard, right in his goddamn plums.

The kick had been nice. After, she'd swiveled on her heel and headed to school, leaving him on his knees. She could feel him holding his tongue while he watched her walk away. London understood immediately that he did this for himself—not for her—so that later he might be proud of how he'd held back, turning his restraint into some sort of atonement or payment for what they'd done. It was a cheap price.

Hers would be higher.

Now London turned off Chelsea onto Bennington, and then crossed the bridge over the tracks. She didn't mind heading to the old lady's house. She'd lived all over Eastie in a hundred shitty places, where she had minded it a lot. Living with old lady Dumas suited her fine.

Thelma Dumas rented a single room on the second floor of a triple-decker. The sink ran only cold water and the room had no toilet, so London and the Missus— as London called the old lady—had to descend a flight of stairs and exit the back door to where an outhouse sat inside a yard surrounded by the ricketiest fence London had ever seen, and she'd lived all her life in East Boston, the land of rickety fences. Otherwise, the room wasn't bad. Its sink was flanked by shelves lined with tins of food and an assortment of cracked dishes. There was also a coal stove that heated the room reasonably well, a table with three chairs, and two beds, one of which London had been sleeping in for three years. Her own bed. Besides a dress, coat, boots, and two pairs of underwear, it was all she could call her own.

Two of the chairs in the room sat on either side of the table, while the third was pulled up close to the room's single window, which overlooked Bennington Street. This chair was where the old lady spent her days, and except for on the very coldest or rainiest, the window was always open. "To blow the stink out of the place," the Missus would grumble.

But London knew it was really open for another reason—so the old woman, perched just inside it, might be able to share her lovely opinions with passersby.

Opinions such as, "The world is going to hell in a handbasket," and "Nobody's listening," and "Shit like this doesn't happen in Chicopee," the small town miles from Boston where the old woman had grown up and thus constantly upheld as the rightest location on earth. Although her favorite opinion, and therefore the one most oft repeated, was, "People are crap."

The neighborhood was overly familiar with Thelma Dumas's opinions, which were mostly ignored. However, London's first few days of being exposed to them were enlightening. A swell of understanding rose within her, and she immediately felt this was the place for her, even if the Missus also believed that London was crap. London tended to agree. She quickly fell into the rhythm of life inside the single room on Bennington Street, staying longer here than she ever had anywhere else. Believing maybe she'd stay forever.

But now London knew her time on Bennington was likely limited. And maybe because of this, she began to notice things, like the way her boots stuck lightly to the greasy stairs as she climbed to the second floor, the crack in the umbrella stand outside Thelma Dumas's door, or the way the old woman's face sagged with sadness sometimes as she sat at the window.

London knew she'd have to tell the old woman eventually. She had little hope the Missus would allow her to stay. But then London had never been the hopeful type. She was fourteen, and it was nearly time for her to leave school for the factories anyway. She'd keep it from the old woman, find a job, and then save her scratch until the job fired her and the old woman most likely kicked her out. Past this, London didn't allow herself to think or plan. Not being the hopeful type, she was also not one to believe things could work out differently from the way she saw them working out all around her every day. Therefore, she knew that this growing being inside her might very well soon be living with her own Thelma Dumas. Still, this stark thought had driven her deep inside herself. Perhaps it was why she didn't notice that the door was ajar when she reached the second floor.

"Run!" the old lady growled, before she was knocked from her chair by an angry silver-haired cop looming over her.

London was so startled by the strange scene that she didn't do anything in that first moment but watch the old woman's head hit the window frame. That was a mistake—London's hands were violently secured together, and she was shoved against the metal frame of the old woman's bed, where she tumbled to the floor and then lay desperately trying to catch her breath.

She could hear the old lady shouting at the men. How many, London couldn't tell. All she could see were boots surrounding the woman's ratty slippers. London struggled to make sense of what was happening. What had she done? What had the Missus done? Besides the old lady's hooch, London could think of nothing. Why would a crowd of bulls be interested in a couple of bottles of illegal whiskey?

The cops dragged the Missus from the floor and tossed her back into her chair. London's head cleared. She could now see there were three cops, making five of them inside the small room, and they seemed to be talking about her. The entire scene was beyond anything London could understand. No one had ever taken any notice of her in her life, except for Alby, and that hadn't turned out so well.

"I told you what would happen if you didn't cooperate, you hag," the silver-haired cop shouted into the old lady's face.

She responded by spitting into his.

London closed her eyes so she wouldn't see it, but she sure as hell heard it, as the woman's head struck the window frame again.

London stumbled to her feet toward the Missus, but one of the badges grabbed a fistful of her hair and dragged her toward the door. London kicked and bit, fighting mightily to keep herself inside the room, but the cop was a genuine baby grand, and with his fist locked in her hair, her body followed her head, her boots scraping across the floor.

The cop stopped abruptly in the doorway, and London, hanging from his hand, finally caught her first solid glimpse of the old lady. Her face was bloodied, her gray hair was a tangled mess, and her dress's collar was ripped off one of her shoulders, but her eyes shone more brightly than the electric streetlamps in Scollay Square.

"This dago bitch is a moron," barked the cop holding

London by the head, and he shook her in response to his words.

"Piss out your ass!" London cried.

London could hear the old lady's cackling laughter over the crack of her own skull against the doorframe, making the pain more than worth it.

"Not only are you a moron," the cop said, turning London's head to face him, "but you're also a knocked-up little slut."

His words struck her harder than her head had hit the doorframe—hearing it like this, out in the open. Pregnant. Yes. She was pregnant. How this man could possibly know, or care, London didn't have time to ponder. She went limp with confusion as the man jerked her out the door. . . . The last thing she saw was the old woman's fists striking out at the gray-haired cop.

London threw herself back toward the room, grasping for the doorframe but only succeeding in slipping off her feet. Her cheek struck the umbrella stand, which spun down the sticky steps, cracking into loud shattering pieces.

"My umbrella stand!" Thelma Dumas screeched. "You broke my stand! That was from Chicopee!"

As London was dragged down the stairs past the shards of clay, the old woman's voice rang in her ears over and over.

"Chicopee! Did you hear me! Chicopee, goddamn it!"

After London was tossed onto the floor of the

waiting police wagon, she could still hear the old lady shouting the word "Chicopee"—that is, until the metal door was slammed and locked, and the vibration of the truck's motor thumped into action beneath her chest.

The gritty floor felt cool against her throbbing cheek. It was dark in the metal box, and the girl in the iron lung sprang back into London's mind. For a moment, London imagined she was there, curled up inside the lung, but then the truck ground into gear and jumped forward.

London leaped to her feet and beat the hell out of the locked door of the police wagon as the vehicle took off toward the tracks.

Later, she wished she'd taken one last look up at that window.

Maxine woke from her dream. She had been there again.

Home.

Maxine often dreamed of home, though home hadn't quite been the stuff of dreams. The shadows of the meatpacking plants of Somerville had been a solemn spot to be born—a spot where reverence and duty reigned, and strict discipline took the place of humor and caresses. But there had been love, too. Even if that love had been rigid and abrupt. How could it not have been, with their mother needing to care for all her brothers?

Lying awake on the cot next to her sister, Rose, Maxine longed for home. It was such a familiar sensation after four years at the institution that it had become as comfortable to her as her dreams. Born just one year apart, she and Rose had been taking care of each other since they were fidgets. Their mother had taught them early that life was responsibility, a world of set routines and conduct. Rose excelled at both; Maxine, neither. Maxine preferred to change what life was, even if only inside her head.

Maxine closed her eyes and listened to rustling sheets, snores and snorts, and the heavy breathing of the dormitory around her, slowly returning to the last scene of her dream. She had been watching her mother as she leaned over the sink, the spot where Maxine best remembered her. Yet instead of her head being bent over the dishes, her mother stared out the small back window into the tangle of weeds behind their rented rooms, where they hung the laundry. Her face stern, and her lips running parallel to the line of worry across her brow, just as they had back then, but Maxine saw something else in those lines. A yearning for her two daughters. Though, her mother knew she couldn't get to them. Not yet. Not now when the boys—so many boys—were still young. But soon. When the cold-water flat wasn't so crowded. When their father wasn't so tired from the packinghouse. Soon. She'd forgive Maxine. And that other expression her mother had worn, the one Maxine never dreamed of, would finally fade from Maxine's memory.

Rose wiggled on the cot, pulling Maxine once again from her dreaming.

"Did the whistle blow?" Rose asked.

"Shhh," Maxine soothed.

"Did it blow, Maxxie?" Her voice echoing across the sleeping dormitory.

Maxine tensed, at once looking around for Ragno

while at the same time searching their narrow cot for Rose's stick.

Alice woke on the cot next to them. Mimicking Maxine, she first checked to see if the night attendant had been roused by Rose. Then she plunged her hand into the small slice of space between their two cots to feel about on the floor for the stick, both girls knowing it was the only thing that would settle Rose.

Alice found it.

She quickly handed it off to Maxine, who had been staring at the dark and empty entrance to the dormitory, as if closely watching it could keep it dark and empty.

Maxine handed the worn maple branch to Rose, who immediately grasped it to her breast, and then reached out and tapped Maxine four times on her chest where her heart was.

"I love you too, Rosy," Maxine whispered. "So very much. Now close your eyes."

Maxine ran her hand softly over her sister's eyes, just as she did almost every night when it came time for bed, hoping that Rose wasn't too much awake to slip back to sleep. Nature seemed to step in and help as the wind jostled the windows of the dormitory and prompted Rose to clutch her stick close and nestle in against her sister, where she drifted quickly off to sleep.

Rose's outburst and the fear of Ragno might have had the power to sweep away any pleasant dreams for the rest of the night for anyone else, but Maxine was a practiced dreamer. It helped that Alice had allowed Maxine to squeeze her fingertips in thanks for finding her sister's stick. Touching was against the rules. Touching Alice was even more against them.

Maxine leaned into Rose and slid right into an old favorite—a day at the beach. Maxine had grown up so close to the sea that she'd been able to smell it on a windy morning, and although she'd never been, this didn't stop her from imagining the waves and the sun and a lingering afternoon that included a picnic. Maxine often dreamed of picnics. Eating on a pretty blanket while the sun warmed your shoulders and birds chirped all around . . . her mother laughing at her brothers playing in the water, and her father napping on the sand. Rose was there, of course, as was Alice.

Alice was always there.

lice woke ten minutes before the whistle blew. She always did. Everything at the Massachusetts School for the Feeble-Minded, where she had spent the last seven years of her life, was on a schedule, including Alice.

A whistle began the day at five thirty in the morning, and the girls were herded into their first session of "excusing," the word used for the sometimes thirty minutes of sitting together on the long row of toilets that all students were made to do periodically during the day. Next came dressing in the clothing room. Then a walk on the circular paths just a short distance from the dormitory, where the weak light of dawn seemed to greet them begrudgingly.

Breakfast succeeded the circles—boiled beef, oatmeal, and milk.

Classroom time, which consisted of any number of activities, none of which had anything to do with a pencil or paper.

Lunch. Always soup and bread and more milk.

Manual Training, which for Alice meant time spent in front of the gears, wheels, and handles of the mangle machines, pressing the water out of bedsheet after bedsheet until dinner, a combination of breakfast and lunch served at three.

Then back they went, for another regulated walk, this time to the beat of a drum. They marched the circular paths until four . . . the hour that brought Alice to her favorite place, the window in the day room.

Today had been like all the others, and Alice had done what she did every day—she'd lived it. Her reward was to find herself on the hard benches of the day room, where they had an hour to sit while waiting for their group's turn in the toilet room to excuse their bladders and bowels, followed by their turn in the clothing room to change their clothes for bed.

Alice's brother had dropped her off at the school on a long-ago summer afternoon. It had been a hot day, but she'd forgotten about the heat while traveling in the automobile. Her first auto ride. He'd borrowed it, and then taken her for candy on Tremont Street. Another first. She'd never tasted anything that came out of a wrapper. After, they'd taken the long eleven-mile drive out into the country, leaving behind the dense streets of the South End, where two of her brothers worked as Pullman porters and the third as a lineman for the railroad, and where she had lived with the eldest of her brothers, and his now-pregnant wife, since the death of her father.

Her brother hadn't explained what they were doing or where they were going, and Alice hadn't asked. Her life had been a series of things she'd had to do—leave school, clean for the neighbors, take care of the children of her brothers—and knowing ahead of time what those things were didn't change anything.

Though Alice didn't ask where they were going, she had a pretty good idea why. A few days earlier, she'd been walking down Columbus Avenue with her brother's wife when a white woman had caught sight of her clubfoot and clicked her tongue, a pretty common reaction to Alice living her life. But then the woman had noticed the large belly of Alice's brother's wife and said, "Pray to the Lord this next one don't come out tainted." And Alice had seen the fear in the young, pregnant woman's eyes.

Less than a week later, Alice and her brother were rolling through the entrance gate and up the curving driveway of the institution, slowly, as if the borrowed automobile itself felt unsure of this decision.

Every so often over the years, something would flash in Alice's mind and she'd see the school again as she had that first day—the massive brick buildings presiding over great expanses of lawn. Alice had never seen so much mowed grass in all her life. It had made her shy. Her brother had taken her hand as they'd climbed the steps, and for the first time that day she understood the seriousness of her situation. He'd never held her hand before; though she'd been limping on a twisted foot all her life, Alice had never needed help walking. It was only later that she realized he'd held it for another reason, because it would be the last time she'd ever see him. Within an hour, Alice would be swept into the moving river of routine that was the institution.

She now sat in the very room and in the very spot where she'd been placed that first day—following a short stop in the small office with her brother and a nurse—next to the front doors of the dormitory, where he'd told her that this was for the best.

Alice now stared out across the darkening lawn and listened to Maxine and Rose chatter, the sweet sound of their voices smoothing out the long day that had coiled up inside her. She was always amazed at how much the two had to say to each other, especially since the pair spent most of the day together. Maxine was her sister's caretaker, and the school matched their classroom and manual-labor schedules, at least until Maxine turned fifteen, which would take place next year . . . for both Alice and Maxine.

At fifteen, school ended at the institution and adult life began. Alice and Maxine would be moved from the girls' dormitory to the women's dormitory. They'd still be called girls, though. All women inmates at the Massachusetts School for the Feeble-Minded— or the Walter E. Fernald State School, as it had now come to be called after the death of the old superintendent—were referred to as girls, whether you were fourteen or forty. No matter the name of the institution, it was a lifetime placement, and no one— no matter the diagnosis—ever left.

Although, it wasn't only age that had the potential to separate the sisters, but the machine of the institution itself. The groupings within the girls' dormitory were now firmly set within the system of the institution. And once set, the machine of the place rattled on, never changing. But if you were scheduled to move into the women's dormitory, who knew what the machine would do? Perhaps it would separate the sisters by diagnoses? Rose had been born a Mongoloid and diagnosed an imbecile. Maxine and Alice had been diagnosed morons. For all Alice knew, morons, imbeciles, idiots, Mongoloids, cripples, epileptics, and so on could be placed into different women's dormitories or cottages across the huge expanse of the institution's grounds. The chances of the machine keeping the sisters together were slim, and slimmer still for keeping Alice and Maxine together. Maxine never spoke about the coming move, or their inevitable separation, but it was all Alice ever thought about.

"Police wagon," Maxine said suddenly.

Alice had been staring out the window but had seen nothing other than the coming darkness. Now she saw the truck with its two dimly shining headlamps making its way toward the girls' dormitory, the same route her brother had driven long ago. It wasn't an uncommon sight, this truck. It had actually grown much more common in the past few years.

"Bet you a nickel this girl is a moron," Maxine said.

"You don't have a nickel." Rose laughed. Rose laughed a lot. As long as she was with Maxine, anyway. "Do you have a nickel, Alice?"

"No, baby," Alice said. "But I wouldn't take that bet because your sister's probably right. The girl's a moron."

Female idiots showed up at Fernald most often in hospital wagons, not police wagons, and were taken straight to the large North Building that housed the Sick Ward. They were the inmates who needed the most care. The doctors at Fernald diagnosed as idiots those who would never grow mentally past the age of two years old. Female imbeciles—Rose's diagnosis—could mentally reach the age of seven, and might end up in either the dormitory or the Sick Ward, depending on whether they were mobiles. Morons were almost always dropped off at the dormitory, and they often showed up in police wagons. Morons could attain the mental age of twelve years old.

When Alice had first arrived, she'd been seven and couldn't believe she would ever be twelve. Double digits. Almost a teenager. Impossible. One of the nurses had told her in the kindest of voices that as a moron, Alice would be able to attain a level of usefulness to society. That long-ago day, Alice had kissed the nurse's hand. Here was a white woman, a nurse, telling her she'd be someone. But by the time Alice had reached double digits, she'd used the shame of that kiss to seal herself away from everyone. Even Maxine.

"If I had a nickel," Rose announced, "I'd bet this girl is going to be my new friend."

Maybe Alice hadn't sealed herself away from *everyone*. No one could seal themselves away from Rose.

As the police wagon made its way to the front steps of the dormitory, it began to rain. The driver stepped out, hatless, his silver hair whipping about in the wind. Another policeman appeared at the back and unlocked it. A moment went by where the men stood in the rain and nothing happened. The silver-haired man howled into the truck, gesturing angrily with his thumb for the person in the back to come out. Its occupant obviously didn't move, and the man was forced to crawl in.

Alice watched with a little more interest.

The cop backed out of the truck, his hand wrapped firmly around the forearm of a girl with wild black hair, her body swinging about like a fish on the end of a short line.

The second cop grabbed her other arm, and she was caught tightly between them. There was nowhere to go, and the girl, realizing it, threw her hair out of her face to catch her first glimpse of the institution.

Rose let out a light groan. "She's hurt."

The girl had a large wound on her cheek, clotted

but fresh, a red bruise swelling up half her face. The men pulled at the girl's arms, but she snapped them back, glaring. And then she walked herself, still cuffed, up the stairs and into the dormitory.

Alice smiled, but only in her mind—something she had learned always to do on the inside of herself, never the outside. *I will bet myself a nickel that this one finds her way out of here within the week.* Four hand claps rang out across the room. The signal. Time to line up for toilets, clothes, and bed.

Lights-out happened at five thirty, no matter if the sun was still streaming through the large dormitory windows or not.

Rose hated bedtime, but she didn't mind toilet time. Toilet time meant water time.

The ladies locked the group of them into the bathroom alone, and Maxine let her play in the sinks. Toilet time came before nightclothes, and so Maxine never cared if Rose got herself sopping wet . . . so Rose got herself sopping wet.

She scrubbed her face, her ears, her neck, and ran water all through her hair while the other girls sat on the toilets.

Of course, she "urinated" or "defecated," as the ladies liked her to call it. She was in the bathroom. It was a good time for this. But then came time at the sink.

Sometimes she'd get her hair really wet, and then toss it over her face and head toward Maxine and Alice, with her arms stretched out in front of her, growling like a monster. Maxine always laughed, but

Alice would tell Rose to pipe down. Alice was afraid of the ladies. Alice was afraid of so many things. Rose understood. She was afraid of stuff too. Like being without her sister. Everything looked different when her sister wasn't in the room.

"Do you think they'll lock her in Twenty-Two for the night?" Maxine asked. She was talking about the girl from out in the rain. The one with the cut on her face.

"Most likely," Alice said.

Rose knew that Alice was usually right. Thinking about the girl being alone in the cages made splashing in the water less fun. Rose had never seen the cages, but all the girls talked about them. They were in the place called Ward Twenty-Two, a place Maxine promised Rose would never go. A place Maxine had never been. Alice had. Bunches of times. For "giving a look" to one or another of the ladies, something only Alice seemed to be able to give, this special look that the ladies hated. And when Alice came back, she sure wouldn't look at anyone, not even Rose.

Rose had begged Alice to tell her about the cages, but all Alice would say was they weren't so bad. She knew Alice didn't like it in the cages. She also knew Alice didn't want to tell her this. But the cages were bad. Rose knew.

Rose knew a lot of things people thought she didn't. She knew she and her sister were in a place for sick people. She knew she and her sister weren't sick, and that most of the kids who surrounded her weren't sick. She knew that some of the ladies who cared for them were kind, and that many of them were not. She knew all about the reports and evaluations and lists and schedules that were kept on everything from how many pounds of laundry were washed each day to who visited on visiting day each month to what kind of attitude she had on a Monday at lunch.

She knew about the fights the bigger girls got into, and also how this place sucked the fight out of them behind closed doors. She knew about the cut-up body parts floating in jars in the back of the Sick Ward, and about the men and women locked forever in the Back Ward of the North Building. Rose knew because she listened, and because she watched. Most especially she watched her class, the twelve girls locked in the bathroom with her right now.

She knew that Lizzie cried at night in her cot because her head—filled with water—ached much more when she lay down. But also that Lizzie liked to eat. And on days when Lizzie's head seemed to bother her most, Rose would steal an extra piece of fruit at dinner to give to Lizzie when they changed for bed in the clothing room. Rose found it easy to steal. All she had to do was smile nicely at the ladies in the dining hall, and then snatch the fruit quickly under her skirt when they turned away. They never suspected her, and she never felt any guilt over it. Rose wasn't the only one who stole things. Everyone did.

The best at it was Frances. Frances had been at the school for as long as Rose, and had a bad case of rheumatism, which made her knees weak and her walk wobbly. She fell constantly, and always had cuts and bruises on her arms and legs. Although, *sometimes* Frances would fall into the bread bowl at dinner, and come away with a few slices that no one saw her take . . . except for Rose. Once, Rose even saw Frances stumble into the collection plate at church. The flash of coins popping into her pocket made Rose laugh right out loud, which caught the attention of the meanest person at the school, the lady called Mrs. Ragno.

"That one is always laughing at nothing," Mrs. Ragno said.

Rose was quick to laugh again, this time at nothing, so the lady would be right. Because another thing Rose knew was that the lady liked to be right. Rose also knew to stay far away from her, and from Bessie and Ellen, who sat on the toilets farthest away from Rose standing at her sink. Bessie and Ellen did terrible things to the girls who the lady was mad at. Rose was afraid of them and closed her eyes whenever they came near. Mostly they attacked Sarah and Neddie. Rose knew it was because Sarah and Neddie behaved the most differently from the others.

Sarah didn't have water in her head like Lizzie or wiggly legs like Frances, but she did things that no one else did, like pull her skirt up over her head whenever the ladies clapped too loudly to call everyone to dinner or toilet. Neddie was a Mongoloid, but unlike Rose, Neddie spoke in a really loud voice that attracted Bessie's and Ellen's attention. Though, anybody could be hurt by Bessie and Ellen, even if you didn't talk too loudly. Rose knew this because Bessie and Ellen hurt her, too.

They only did it when Maxine and Alice weren't watching, like during shoe shine time or when Maxxie helped Alice run the mangles. Bessie and Ellen would drag Rose into some corner and quietly knee her, over and over and over . . . sometimes until Rose thought she would be killed. But it always stopped. Eventually. And then Rose would wait until they were gone, crawl out of the corner, and wipe all the tears and snot off her face so Maxine and Alice wouldn't know.

Maxine could never know. Rose definitely knew this. To tell Maxine would be bad. It's what Bessie and Ellen wanted her to do.

The only girls Bessie and Ellen never physically attacked were Alice and Mary. Alice said it was because they were Negroes. Rose knew Alice was right. Rose could tell that the brown color of Alice's and Mary's skin made Bessie and Ellen afraid of them. Rose's skin was the color of most everybody else's at the school, including Bessie's and Ellen's, so they weren't scared of it. She often wished these girls would just disappear. But there were so many things to wish for at the Fernald School, like wishing Lizzie's head didn't hurt her so much, or that the ladies served

Bit-O-Honeys for breakfast, or that she could wear a red dress sometimes . . . one with a long, flowy sash, and a—

"Rose!"

Rose pulled her hands from the drain and jumped back from the overflowing sink, her boots sopping wet.

"Clean it up," Bessie barked from her broken toilet seat. Bessie was always the one to talk. Never Ellen. Which made Rose more afraid of Ellen.

Rose scuttled over to Maxine while Alice went for the mop.

"Sorry, sorry, sorry," Rose whispered into her sister's ear, squishing her wet body in between the wall and the toilet.

"Oh, Rosy," Maxine sighed.

"It's just water, Maxine," Alice said.

"Shut your trap and mop it up," Bessie growled.

Rose kept her eyes closed, but she could hear from Bessie's voice that she was still on her toilet and not heading toward them, meaning she probably wasn't in the mood to be punching today.

The key clicked in the lock, and all the girls stood up from the toilets. Rose opened her eyes and let go of her breath. It was time for bed. She hated bed.

Following behind Alice and in front of Maxine on the way to the clothing room, Rose remembered the girl with the hurt face.

"Is that girl going to the cages tonight, Alice?" Rose asked.

But before Alice could answer, they entered the clothing room and there she was. The girl. Standing in nightclothes, her long, black hair still dripping from the rain, and a bandage stuck across her cheek.

Bessie walked right up to the girl and bumped her hard with her shoulder. Rose ducked behind Maxxie. She couldn't watch.

"Those are my nightclothes, wop," Bessie said in her low, mean voice.

"Back off or I'll paste you."

It was the girl with the cut on her face. Talking to Bessie. Without even a tiny shake or quiver in her voice.

Rose clenched her left hand into a fist against her chest and tapped on her forehead with her right hand. Four times. Then four times. Then four times.

Bessie wouldn't do it now. She'd do it in secret. Where no one could see.

Tonight. Tomorrow. Soon.

That girl was going to get it.

London had seen enough. She wasn't staying. Not even the night. She couldn't have cared less about the big girl with the thick bangs who'd sized her up. Or her white-haired friend with the lightest blue eyes London had ever seen—so light that the dark centers of them stood out and made the girl look like a corpse. Two pieces of shit like that, London could handle. It wasn't as if she hadn't been jumped before— dozens of times—on the street, inside orphanages, and in just about every house she'd been fostered in. Being beat on wasn't that bad . . . compared to what else could happen. But if those girls came with a crowd, she might have trouble. She had to think about the baby.

The baby.

That's what the nurse in the office kept calling it. London hadn't stopped thinking about her situation since the morning she'd vomited into the gutter, but she'd never thought about it this way—as an actual child that might be born.

"The baby will come in June. Do you understand?" the nurse had asked.

Since London wasn't sure yet of anything in this new place, she had nodded instead of telling the woman to go suck off a dog—the old lady would have enjoyed that one. But thinking about the Missus also meant thinking about the sound of the old lady's head hitting the window frame, and the last moment before London was dragged away. London was going to make those scrubs pay for what they did . . . once she got out of here.

The nurse had proceeded to poke about on her, studying and taking notes. She'd peered into London's mouth and ears, and asked her strange questions, like could London give three differences between a king and a president. London had looked around her for the first time and realized she was in a kind of hospital, and not a hospital for her busted cheek.

"I don't know any kings or presidents."

"Is that your answer?" the nurse had asked.

London had attempted to gauge whether or not answering correctly would change her circumstances. She decided it wouldn't. Or at least not by much. Maybe if she cooperated with the nurse's idea of who London was, she wouldn't be placed under as much supervision.

"Yes," she'd told the nurse.

"Please tell me what is similar between a snake, a cow, and a sparrow."

"They're animals."

The nurse scribbled away for quite some time. London had meant to get that one correct and was pretty sure she had. What could this woman be writing?

The nurse finally raised her head. "I'm going to read a few sentences that have something foolish in them, some bit of nonsense. I want you to listen carefully and tell me what is foolish about each one. Are you ready?"

London nodded. According to her hastily formed plan of answering every other question correctly, she was supposed to get this next one wrong. But she sat up straighter in her chair and waited for the question like she wanted to answer it correctly. Did she want to answer it correctly?

"The first sentence is: *An engineer said that the more cars he had on his train, the faster he could go.* What is foolish about this?"

"Is the train moving downhill?"

"Is this your answer?"

"It was a question," London said, feeling very much like she wanted to sock this woman.

London usually liked quizzes and tests in school. She did well on them. School had always been a place where London felt right, although she kept this to herself. She didn't want any of the teachers expecting anything. Learning occupied London's mind in the same way fighting did: it took up all the space inside her, making her feel strong and in control; learning just entailed less blood and busted teeth than fighting.

"Yes, my dear. It was a question," the nurse said. "And I need your answer."

"The question is foolish. That's what is foolish."

"Is that—"

"Yes," London interrupted. "That is my answer."

"Next question. *Yesterday the police found the body of a girl cut into eighteen pieces. They believe that she killed herself.* What is foolish about this?"

"She was obviously murdered by a butcher."

"Is that your answer?"

London answered the rest of the nurse's questions without bothering with whether or not she was getting them correct. Instead she focused on not planting her fist into this woman's face and taking off. She'd seen there were no guards standing outside the building, and none down by the open gate. But it was a bad plan, running now. She'd be too easy to spot in the daylight.

At the end of the interview, the nurse announced that London appeared to be, "healthy and without marked physical defects, and although wild and unmanageable upon arrival, was now considerably calmed. However, the test plainly shows you to be a high-grade moron, as well as a menace to the community due to your sex interests and lack of self-restraint. I'll have the doctor take a look at my results and confirm tomorrow. For tonight, let's get you settled in."

London didn't give a damn what this nurse thought she was or wasn't. All she cared about was convincing the nurse she was harmless, which she had succeeded in doing. That was why she was being lined up in a group of other girls about her age instead of being locked up in some cellar. London had often been locked in cellars.

A woman attendant walked them out of the room full of clothes and into a room full of beds. It was a queer hour for bed, but this was a queer place. London didn't think too much on it, except to keep her eyes away from the attendant. A woman like that could ruin her escape plan.

London noticed they were on the second floor that faced the front of the building, and that there looked to be three or more other rooms full of beds besides the one she had been led into. Each room held about fifteen girls. Her group included the two thugs London already felt were the only reason to stay the night, so she could play about with them some tomorrow. The Missus would have had *opinions* on these two. Alby hated when London got into fights. As the son of a prosperous butcher, the only blood on his hands came from the daily slaughter. But the old woman had admired London for it. Always muttering how she wished she could get a look at "the other palooka." She understood London in a way Alby never would.

London sighed as she filed into the room in line with the other girls, knowing she couldn't return to

Bennington Street for at least a night or two. She'd have to bust out and then find someplace to hide—let them think she'd kicked it in a ditch somewhere. She remembered it was Wednesday, and figured by Sunday the world would return to not caring two shits about her.

London was shown to a cot near the window, which was perfect. She'd already scoped out the front of the building and noted the gas pipes. It was late October, but London could tell they weren't heating this dump before they absolutely had to. The grass was cut nice, and the brick buildings loomed, large and impressive, but the wet holes in the ceiling of the hallways upstairs and the worn-out boots on the feet of the girls who lived here had not gone unnoticed by her. They weren't overspending in this joint, especially where people weren't looking.

The girls all climbed wordlessly onto their cots. London had spent a considerable amount of time in orphanages, and so knew that the attendant walking up and down the main row was the cause of the silence. London made sure to keep her eyes down. She didn't want to capture the attention of this one.

There was a tension in the air as the attendant stood in the center of the room, and all the girls lay still on their cots, and London tried to figure out what they were waiting for. She pretended to close her eyes, knowing the eyes of the attendant were focused on her.

A loud whistle blew, but London didn't move. She'd

known something was about to happen and would be damned if she'd react and give pleasure to this woman, even if it cost her a scowl. It was worth it. After another minute, the woman lost interest and walked out of the room, locking the door behind her.

The key hadn't finished twisting in the lock when the girl in the cot next to London poked up her head like a rat from its hole.

"Hi."

Her bedmate immediately yanked her back down.

London figured the bedmate was a night-crawler. They existed in almost every place where London had ever closed her eyes to sleep, creeping over in the night and demanding things from you. Night-crawlers always preyed on the weak. And the smiling girl was a Mongoloid.

The girl's head popped up again, the smile already large on her face, but she didn't even get the chance to push the *H* sound out of her mouth before the other girl again pulled her back down.

"Rose, it's time to sleep."

Her voice was kind. She wasn't a night-crawler. Although, whoever she was, she wouldn't look at London. Instead she wrapped her arm around her bedmate and pulled her in close, protectively. And then she reached out and gently ran her hand down the face of the girl she had called Rose, shutting her eyes.

As soon as her hand had passed over Rose's lids,

Rose's eyes popped back open, reminding London of what she'd once seen corn do when set on a hot coal stove, and London actually laughed.

Now another head popped up . . . from the cot on the other side of the two girls. The Negro girl's stare couldn't be missed, along with its meaning. But just in case London hadn't understood, the girl then *pointedly* stared at the door to the dormitory where the attendant had exited.

London rolled her eyes at her. She didn't need to be told what not to do. She knew she shouldn't have laughed. But this Rose was funny.

The girl laid back down with a light thump.

London needed to get the hell out of here. But it was still so light out, even with the rain. Why were they all in bed at half past five in the afternoon? She settled in with a sigh and tried not to look over at Rose looking over at her from her cot, although it was tough, since they were less than a foot from each other, and that little bird wouldn't stop staring.

London broke down and turned to face Rose.

Rose went absolutely wiggly.

Her bedmate gave her an annoyed bump from behind. A warning. Rose opened her eyes more widely and smiled even more brightly at London. Then she slowly began to pull something out from under the covers to show London. It looked like a stick from a tree. And when it emerged, London saw that it was a stick, a very worn stick. The girl hugged it closely to herself, showing London how much she loved it.

A bed creaked across the room, and London gestured with her chin for the girl to hide her stick. In places like this, things that were loved needed to be hidden. Rose immediately buried her stick under the blanket, and London saw that the girl understood how things worked.

The movement alerted Rose's bedmate, who turned around in the cot without disturbing a single coil in the sloping mattress. She whispered something into Rose's ear and gently ran her hand over the girl's eyes again, this time more slowly than the last. But as soon as her hand reached Rose's cheeks, Rose reopened her eyes, and so the bedmate repeated it, over and over, like she was gently washing Rose's face. London noticed how the bedmate never looked over at her. London understood, and didn't take offense. This girl was protecting herself. She didn't know London, but she obviously cared greatly about Rose, and needed to focus on keeping her safe. Probably not an easy job in a place like this. As if on cue, London heard the big brute with the bangs cough meaningfully.

Sighing, London turned over in her cot in an attempt to help the girl put Rose to sleep.

She now looked directly into the wall under the window. If she looked up, she could see the very tops of trees waving in the evening breeze. It looked a little cold out there, and it was still raining, which was far from swell because London would soon be out there, and the sleeping clothes they'd given her were worn thin and she had no shoes. No matter. As soon as it was dark, she was blowing this joint.

She closed her eyes. A weariness came over her. She'd felt it before—it was part of her condition—as if the day's events had been thrown over her like a heavy blanket pinning her to the sagging mattress. She wouldn't allow herself to sleep, because she might be jumped—or, worse, wake up in the morning still locked up in this hole.

The old woman's bloodied face appeared in her mind. She put it out. Thelma Dumas could take care of herself.

London rolled onto her back, careful not to place her hands anywhere near her stomach. She refused to acknowledge her situation yet. It wasn't time.

But now Alby's face came to her, hovering over her as it had that night in the basement of his father's shop, staring into her face as if he'd never seen anything like it before. She wondered why she'd let him. But she knew it was that interested look in his eyes.

When they'd finished, he'd nestled warmly against her on top of a pile of clean aprons, and together they'd watched through the tiny basement window the foot traffic tramping down Decatur Street. It was then that she'd told him about her name. So many people had asked her why a little Italian girl from south in the boot had been named "London."

Her answer had always been that her grandmother was English, and had been born in London, and thus her parents had named her for her grandmother's birthplace. London was too dark-skinned to say her father was English, and she also didn't like creating a picture of her father that wasn't true, since the only picture she had of him was blurry enough. But an English grandmother, this seemed reasonable.

In any case, it was a lie. And that night, lying next to Alby with his eyes staring brightly into hers, she'd told him the truth—that she'd been named for the street they'd found her wandering on in East Boston.

London Street. Only a few blocks away from the old woman's house.

Of course, London didn't remember it. Any of it. Unlocking the door, walking down the three flights of stairs, stepping out into the cold winter day, leaving her mother lying alone, dead in a rented room so very far away from everyone she'd ever known. London almost never thought about it more than to know she'd most likely been hungry, that it probably had been a while since she'd eaten. She'd left her mother to find food. Anyone would do this, whether they were four years old or fourteen. And so instead of "Angeline" or "Simone" or "Filomena," a little Italian orphan had become "London."

Alby had kissed her then. Hard. And they'd done it again.

Afterward, lying there, sweaty and tangled in butcher aprons, he'd wondered aloud what her real name was. This was something London never did.

Now she glanced to her right. Rose was sound asleep, the tip of her stick poking her gently in the cheek. London stared at the back of the girl next to Rose. After a few moments London could detect the slight movement of her steady breath. She was also asleep. Slowly, slowly, London sat up on her cot. It wasn't until she was fully upright that she scanned the room.

It was dark now, finally. Although, there was still a twinge of light around the edges of the world. As her eyes adjusted, London could make out the sleeping forms of the girls tossed every which way across their cots. She knew exactly where the girl with the bangs slept, next to her ghostly friend, and London took her time watching them until she was sure they were asleep.

It had only been an hour or so since the lights had gone out, but London understood the strong effect of routine. Many of these girls had likely lived here most of their lives, and so falling asleep on demand was something they'd grown used to. She couldn't wait to get out of this place.

Barefooted, she stood up and rolled her blanket up as tightly as she could, and then stuffed it under her nightdress. It would come in handy out there in the cold, rainy night. Leaning close to the large window, she attempted to ease it open, needing to use all her might to move it just an inch. *Damn*, she thought. This wasn't going to be so easy.

She turned toward the door, scanning the many beds. No one moved. But the door was locked. She was sure the attendant was not sitting behind it, but probably smoking or bumping somewhere, since she hadn't struck London as the nurturing type, to stick around to be sure the girls slept safely and soundly. Still, busting the door open would bring people running, like the bitch with the bangs and her ghoul.

London turned back to the window and tried again. She got it open another inch. At this rate, she could probably squeeze through in another hour or so. She softly sat down on the bed.

Feeling a tiny tug on her shirt, London swung round, fists up. But it was Rose, peering with wide eyes from under her covers.

London quickly put her finger to her lips to shush her. She saw instantly that the girl wasn't going to make a sound. Instead Rose pointed a finger to her own chest, and then pointed the same finger at the window.

London sucked in a quick breath. The girl wanted to help.

London glanced over at the sleeping body next to Rose. She replayed the memory of this girl gently putting Rose to sleep. It was her sister lying next to her. London knew that if she allowed Rose to help, she'd be putting the girl in danger. That is, if Rose could even climb out of bed without waking her sister, which London doubted.

Rose opened her eyes a tiny bit wider, asking again to help London.

Anger wrapped itself around London's heart like a cold fist and squeezed. She didn't want help. She didn't want kindness. Life was crap and she liked it that way. It was easier.

She pursed her lips at Rose and shook her head, causing the girl to frown.

Shit.

London quickly pointed to her arm and made a muscle, showing Rose how strong she was, and the girl smiled. Damn it if that girl's grin wasn't kippy, and though London embraced the anger humming through her body, she couldn't stop her mouth from curling slightly up at its corners.

Rose then removed her arm from her covers and pointed across the room.

London turned to look at—the moon? She turned back, a questioning look on her face.

Rose pointed behind London at the window she'd just tried to open, followed by a thumbs-down. She then pointed again across the room and gave a thumbs-up.

Now London understood. Rose was telling her the window across the room opened more easily. Without thinking, London reached out, grabbed Rose's small hand, and squeezed it in her larger one. Besides Alby, she'd never willingly touched anyone before in her life. The strangeness shocked her, and she quickly let the girl go and started for the window.

It opened as easily as if it'd been greased. London was out, down the gas pipe, and running across the cold, wet grass in a flash. She never looked back at Rose, just as she'd never looked back at the old woman. It didn't matter. In the next two days she'd be home.

And Rose, with her pretty grin, would be a memory.

lice noticed the open window the second she woke. She quickly shut her eyes. To be the first one to notice, to call out the alarm, could implicate her in the elopement. Even if they believed she had nothing to do with it, she'd still spend the day inside someone's office explaining the fact that she had nothing to do with it . . . and they'd all be writing, writing, writing in those notebooks. The doctor, the nurse, the matron, the attendant, all scribbling away about her. Recording what?

Everything. They recorded everything. How loose her bowel movements were. How often she dragged her foot when walking the morning circle. How quickly she ate her soup.

When Alice had been ten and the nurse had left her alone in the room, she'd snatched a sheet from one of the files on the desk. It was the only thing she'd ever stolen. She'd stuffed the page into her underwear and quickly sat back down. The nurse returned, and Alice blinked at her as she always did, with perhaps a few extra blinks. The nurse didn't notice the extra blinks or the missing page, which struck Alice as funny. Not that she'd ever laugh. It wasn't something Alice did.

Later that day during a session of Domestic Training, which just meant changing the diapers of the low-grades, Alice had crouched behind one of the beds and read.

Brother is a laborer. Home fair to inferior. Parents both dead. A hasty examination shows that Alice has no scholastic ability. She is burdened with a defective foot, and there are suspicions of constitutional inferiority. Alice is a child troubled by unhappy thoughts who seems to have a great capacity for sorrow. She can remember vividly all that happens in her day, recalling these scenes with great exactness. Had she been normal, one feels she might have been clever. She is also rather good-looking if one does not hunt for appearances of intelligence. Alice will develop but little further. Belongs at about the middle-grade to high-grade moron.

The special training we can offer Alice will no doubt be of great benefit to her, but no training can supply the mental fiber that is lacking, and whatever improvement may result, the expense and the trouble are thrown away if the child, later on, is tossed out into the world without being able to protect and care for herself. Therefore, protection, shelter, and care of Alice must be lifelong and permanent.

Flipping the paper over gave Alice the measurements of the circumference of her head, the length of her arms, her legs, her fingers. They'd measured everything, even the crushed toes on her right foot. The paper had her weight . . . her eye color . . . her bust size . . . the shade of her teeth. . . . Alice ripped it to shreds. Tiny, tiny shreds. Shreds that she plucked from the floor and stuffed into the old diaper from an inmate she hadn't yet washed. She tried not to count the shreds, but it was as if she had to. She counted each and every one, wrapped that number she would never forget inside the diaper, and tossed it into the dark water of the soaking bucket.

Now, with Alice lying on her cot, the morning whistle blew.

Alice kept her eyes closed. She wouldn't be the first person the morning attendant, Miss Sweeney, saw when she noticed that the window was open and the girl was missing. Alice waited until she heard the gasps, the commotion, and then she stretched and slowly opened her eyes.

Maxine was looking straight ahead, her features loose and relaxed. Alice did the same. Rose was still asleep. Alice could see the tip of her stick poking out from under the covers. Maxine had forgotten it in the midst of all the screaming Miss Sweeney was doing as she called out over and over again to the matron on the first floor. It would be blamed on Miss Sweeney, this elopement. Part of her job as night attendant was to bed-check every hour. Alice was a few feet away, but the girl's bed looked quite cold. She hadn't slipped out a half hour earlier.

Alice cleared her throat. Maxine's hand moved to Rose's stick and hovered over it, waiting. As soon as Miss Sweeney ran from the room, Maxine dropped to her knees between the cots, plucked the stick from the covers, and slipped it into the heating vent. Then she gently roused Rose, who woke up smiling, until she heard the screaming, at which time she clutched at Maxine.

"Out of bed!" the matron shouted. "All of you. Out of bed. Now!"

The girls sprang from their cots. They understood the drill. This was certainly not the first elopement at the school, and it wouldn't be the last. They'd all spend the morning sitting the benches for sure.

Alice had never thought of running. So many had. Some had made it. More had not. But it wasn't the statistics that kept Alice from ever considering it. She had no place to go and no money to go with. Every inmate knew you needed clams and a sandbar—money and an address. Without these two things, a runner got caught, dragged back, and thrown into the cages.

The girls shivered at the ends of their beds. The window that the girl with the wild hair had escaped through had not been closed, and the cold morning chill that had left a wet film on the glass now made its way through their threadbare sleeping clothes.

Dottie made the mistake of picking up her blanket and wrapping it around herself. The matron swiftly had Dottie's ear between her fingers and was pulling her out of the room.

"The rest of you. Get dressed. You'll be spending the day on the benches."

No one so much as twitched their lips into a frown, let alone groaned, but Alice could feel every heart in the room falling. It would be ten long hours of sitting still. Alice finally risked a glance over at Maxine. Their eyes met. The benches inevitably meant more bad things would be happening today.

They sat the benches in the day room until half past six, at which time they were herded first into the toilet room to take care of their business and next into the dining room, where they were given just enough time to gulp down their breakfast. Then it was back to the benches of the day room . . . with almost four hours to sit before lunch.

With the girls lined up, feet on the floor, eyes straight ahead, backs against the hard wood, the minutes did not move quickly. To make sure everyone knew this, a large clock with the loudest ticking Alice had ever heard had been placed over the entry to the room, so even if you couldn't see it from your position on the bench, you could hear it, slowly ticking each second of every minute.

You didn't get to choose your position on the bench like you did for the hour they normally spent in this room each afternoon. Instead you were placed on it, except for Maxine and Rose, Helen and Sarah, and Edwina and Neddie. If you were in charge of a low-grade, you always had to be next to her. Although as soon as Miss Sweeney turned her back, the girls silently moved to the places where they wanted to be and the people they wanted to be next to. When the attendant returned, she never noticed the difference. They were all "girls" and were all "lined up on benches," which is how she'd left them. Girls. Inmates. Idiots. Imbeciles. Morons. Undesirable. Feebleminded. All interchangeable. All degenerates.

Alice snuck a peek at Maxine. She didn't want to catch the girl's attention because if Maxxie was quietly dreaming, which she looked to be, it was best to let her stay in her head, and not remind her of the hours and hours they had left to sit.

Rose sat between them tapping her thigh lightly with her pointer finger. Tap, tap, tap, tap. One, two, three, four. It was a sequence Alice was familiar with. Rose did it all the time. She tapped things four times before she ate them. If she brushed up against you by accident, she'd quickly tap you there three more times in the same manner. It was just part of Rose. Alice had seen her do it when she was distressed, but she'd also seen Rose tap Maxine's heart four times in moments of joy. She seemed especially nervous today, but then again, sitting the benches made them all nervous.

What did Rose's file say? Did they know about the tapping? Alice was sure they did. They seemed to know about everything . . . everything but maybe where that black-haired girl was.

Someone touched Alice's shoulder.

Maxine.

She had reached over the top of her sister, and then swiftly removed her hand when Alice turned toward her. But Alice could still feel the lingering warmth near her neck where Maxine's fingers had been.

There had once been a time when Alice would have suffered from that touch for days. Now she allowed it to sink deep inside her like a soothing balm. Not that Alice allowed either reaction to escape, so when Maxine smiled at her, silencing the incessant ticking of the clock and relieving the deep ache of Alice's spine against wood, Alice only blinked back.

Following lunch and periodic excusing, Mrs. Ragno replaced Miss Sweeney, and since Ragno wasn't in trouble for allowing an elopement *and* was more interested in hearing the gossip from the other staff about what had happened the night before than in a bunch of girls sitting on benches, the girls began to exchange a few whispers. They were careful not to take advantage. Well, maybe Neddie did, but Ragno was slightly used to Neddie's voice, which helped to shield their whispers.

"Do you think she made it?" Maxine asked.

"If not this time," Alice said, "next time."

Alice was sure of it. That girl had a hard look in her eyes. She would make it. Alice had hoped it all morning. She always hoped that anyone who ran made it. It meant the institution was wrong. The doctors were wrong. The nurses and matron and attendants were wrong. And the girl with wild black hair was out there. Not in here . . . under the protection, shelter, and care of a state school established for idiots, imbeciles, and morons.

Lifelong. And permanent.

London's entire body was shaking with cold, except for her feet, which she couldn't feel. She'd run for about three hours straight. Mostly through the woods. Not feeling her feet as she'd tumbled over rocks and waded knee deep through slippery wet leaves had been a good thing. But now, curled up under her dirty hospital blanket in the back of someone's toolshed, her frozen feet had begun to ache like a bastard.

It was early afternoon. She'd heard activity in the house that belonged to the toolshed, but no voices. London hadn't gotten up to investigate. She lay on the dirt floor only partially hidden behind a stack of broken wooden boxes, shovels dangling overhead. It smelled nice, though, the dirt. Clean. The air, too. She'd never been out in the woods like this, like last night, surrounded by so many trees. Except for the freezing-cold part of the experience, she had enjoyed herself, and she looked forward to being out there again. As soon as it got dark.

By tonight they'd feel less sure about where she could be and would begin searching a wider area. They might even have given up by then. Although, tonight she'd have to figure out where the hell she was.

She lay her head back down on her arm and listened to the cooing and scratching of chickens in the yard. God, her feet ached, and she had to piss harder than a rainstorm. She rolled to her side and tried to think about something other than feet and pissing.

She thought about Rose. How that kid could smile.

She knew she'd put Rose and the others in a jam by running. They were being punished for it right now, she was sure. It was how those places worked—how they always worked. Putting the bitch with the bangs in trouble warmed London's heart. Putting Rose in trouble didn't. She hoped that little trinket could keep from spilling about the window.

London sighed. Worrying about that girl made the pee feel like it was pressing against her teeth. She couldn't wait anymore.

Crawling unsteadily to her knees, London slowly returned her feet to life. The shed didn't have a window, but it wasn't built tightly, as the cold air streaming in all last night could attest to. Choosing an especially large crack between the planks, she peered out into the yard. Her view was about a ten-foot expanse, which included the back door of the house.

There was no one.

After standing back and taking in a few breaths, she slowly pushed the shed door open. There was the lightest of squeaks, but nothing that the warble of the chickens didn't drown out. London now had a total view of the gray clapboard house, the overgrown lawn, the sagging, empty laundry line, and the ripped curtains hanging in the dirty windows. The only things moving were the chickens.

She swooped out the door and closed it ever so quietly, then sped around the side of the shed until she was completely behind it. Wasting no time, she squatted and was in absolute heaven while she gazed out over an empty cornfield. But then someone sneezed.

She stood, back against the shed.

There was a loud squeak of hinges and then the slam of the shed door.

"Goddamn it," someone whispered. Another loud squeak as the door opened again, and this time stayed open.

London didn't move. She listened to the man bumping about inside. But then, silence. She craned her neck, trying to hear what was happening.

Nothing. Nothing was happening. This wasn't good.

Footsteps left the shed and headed for the house.

Shit.

London darted around the shed to the next corner and caught sight of an old man hurrying toward his back door. He was carrying her blanket.

Shit. Shit. Shit.

Without another thought, she bolted for the field. And in less than thirty seconds tripped over a broken stalk of corn, and hit the wet dirt hard. Back up, she was running again. Knees jutting up high into the air so that she'd avoid another fall. Her chest heaved, and her breath rasped loudly in her ears. Had he seen her? Was he chasing her right now? She kept running. Everything a blur. The sun. The sky. The stalks. The brown, muddy earth. She ran for the tree line, which never seemed to grow any closer.

A shot rang out.

London dropped to the ground and lay there. Her heart pounded against the dried cornstalks.

She wasn't shot. It had been a warning.

Slowly she turned her head and looked back. There he was, standing on his back porch, shotgun in his hands, her blanket thrown over his shoulder. She judged the space between them to be more than a hundred yards, his age to be at least seventy, and the tree line close enough anyway. He couldn't do it.

Up she leaped.

He shot again, but this time London didn't fall to the ground. She kept on running. She made the tree line and disappeared into the shadows.

About twenty yards in she stopped to think and catch her breath. The man didn't have many neighbors, and she hadn't seen an auto. It would take him a while to raise an alarm, but London knew the first thing he would do was describe how she'd taken off into these woods.

She had to go back. She had to head out in the opposite direction.

London turned toward the tree line she'd just about killed herself to reach. She approached it slowly. She could make out the house and the back steps but didn't see him. He was most likely on his way to report her. The field was long and wide. She'd have to walk along its edges to bypass the house. She couldn't risk walking out in the open. He might still be there, shotgun ready.

She started to her right, but her eyesight did a funny thing, mixing up the sky and the ground so that she had to reach out and steady herself on a tree. Her vision cleared, but her heart beat heavily, and she was forced to sit on a fallen branch.

It was hunger. That was it. She couldn't remember the last time she'd eaten. She looked up at the house and frowned.

Could she do it?

London was no stranger to stealing. Food, mostly. Sometimes clothes when she needed them. She wondered if that old man lived alone.

London crept back toward the house, keeping watch for any movement. She saw none. The old coot must have taken off to bring in a posse. London drew closer, the thought of food and water driving her through the trees like a lion stalking prey.

She reached the line of trees closest to the house. There were at least twenty yards of open land between herself and the back door. Had he locked it? Her stomach growled. If so, she'd just have to break the window.

Stepping out into the open was a little harder than she'd thought it would be. She hesitated for a good ten seconds, but there was no way around it, and out she darted. If he was in the house, her ham was smoked.

The door was unlocked!

She couldn't believe her luck. It opened into a kitchen, messy but thankfully empty of an old geezer with a gun. London filled a dirty cup with water from the faucet and gulped it so fast, she got the hiccups. There was a pot of cannellini beans sitting on the stove, not her favorite, but she shoveled them into her mouth with her hand, not bothering to look for a spoon. She choked down the beans as she searched the room for more food.

There was a small piece of stale bread on the table. She rolled it up into her sleeve for later and drank down another cup of water. It was time to get the hell out of there.

London opened the back door, and there he was. Waiting. A single thought ran through her mind as the butt of his shotgun smacked her in the forehead.

People are crap.

Maxine could see a sliver of the front gate through the window in the wall to her right from where she sat on the bench. She was, of course, checking out every car, truck, or wagon that pulled through. From years of watching inmates run, she knew that if the girl was going to be caught, it would most likely be today. But she was also imagining that the wide iron gate was the entrance to her home—a large estate, somewhere far out from the city. An estate with grand gardens and fireplaces so massive, they took up entire walls. And dogs. There would be dogs, three of them. No, four. Four large dogs that slept with her in a giant bed every single night.

Motion caught her eye.

A maintenance truck rumbled through her sliver. Not a police vehicle.

She relaxed.

It wasn't that Maxine rooted for the runners; more

than anything, she wished they wouldn't do it in the first place because she hated the aftermath. Watching them dragged back, dirty, often bloody, and always wild with hunger and fear, only to be tossed into Twenty-Two. Days later they would emerge, as gray and flat as the dingy sheets that Alice sent through the gas mangle one after another in the laundry building every afternoon during Manual Training.

And they always seemed to be dragged back.

Making it out obviously took more than "clams and a sandbar," as the girls liked to say. It also took someone who cared about you. So when that truck or wagon pulled up, and the eloper was ripped from it, the world made its pronouncement. *No one cared.* And somehow, *no one* always wore the face of Maxine's mother standing in a dirty alley in Somerville.

Maxine shivered and glanced at Alice's profile without moving. They were not allowed to move. As heavily as the elopers who failed weighed on Maxine, she knew that Alice took their failure much, much harder.

Alice had never tried to run—at least, not in the four years that Maxine had been at the state school. Alice never even spoke of it. Whether this was because she never thought about it or because she understood that Maxine couldn't run, Maxine didn't know. But she hoped that Alice never thought about running, because it would mean leaving her.

An automobile caught Maxine's eye. It wasn't a

police wagon, and she flicked her eyes forward, spotting Alice watching her face. Since Alice was closer to the window, making it impossible for her to see the gate or the driveway without completely turning her head, she'd been using Maxine's expression to determine if the girl had been found.

Before Maxine could go back to deciding on the names of her four dogs, another auto slid through the gate. This time it was a police wagon.

Maxine stiffened, keeping her eyes trained forward, trying not to alert Alice. Maybe it was someone else being brought in for the first time. Maybe there'd been a fight in one of the Back Wards and the police were needed. Maybe . . . Maxine's mind spun, dreaming up a host of reasons why that wagon would enter through the gate, other than the one she knew to be true. It was the girl. And not being able to change this hard fact, she let go of the maybes, allowing Alice to see it. She could never lie to Alice. Or at least, almost never.

Alice saw. So did Rose.

"If not this time, next time," Rose whispered, echoing Alice's own words back at her.

Maxine pushed her thigh against her sister's. Rose always knew the right thing to say. Always. Even on that awful day when their mother had sent them away, and Maxine—sobbing so hard that she could barely speak—had tried to tell Rose she'd get them home. She'd fix it. Rose had simply said, "I believe you," stopping the ache faster than if her little sister had been able to massage Maxine's heart in her small, warm hands.

Maxine didn't expect Alice to respond to Rose, and she didn't. The first thing any one of them learned inside the institution was to hold on to yourself tightly because someone was always watching, and writing it down, creating a slippery path with no way to regain your footing. First they said you were nervous. Then they noted how you seemed agitated. If this upset you, they scribbled more—you were wild, unmanageable even. A menace.

It was enough to turn anyone into a headbanger, one of the little ones who banged their foreheads against the floor over and over again, tenderizing their tiny brains. The action made perfect sense to Maxine. What made no sense at all was a doctor who, when watching these tiny creatures attempting to feel something inside a place that forbade it, had casually told a visitor, "Idiots of the lowest grade seem to have no feelings at all."

The girl hadn't made it, but Alice wouldn't bang her head over it. She would only blink.

It made Maxine want to reach out and touch her, really touch her . . . to place her whole palm against Alice's cheek and feel the light brushing of Alice's lashes against her fingers. Maybe even whisper into her ear that it would be okay. Because sometimes Maxine actually believed this—that eventually, just as she'd told Rose, she'd think up a way of fixing it. But

Maxine did not reach out. Could not. This connection, it was impossible. Although, she often wondered what made it so—the strict rules of this place, or Alice?

There was now a ripple circulating around the day room. Everyone was discovering the news. With so many voices peppering the air, Ragno stepped in from the hallway.

"Quiet!"

The girls immediately shut their mouths.

Ragno had been around for many years, first as Miss Delgorio, and then as Mrs. Ragno, after she'd married one of the mathematics teachers. But under either name, she was serious trouble if her eye fell on you. Of course, anyone at the institution could be trouble for the girls—from the superintendent on down to the men who cut the grass. Maxine had once seen a girl toss a rock at a maintenance man in frustration and be carted off overnight to Twenty-Two, while an hour later when an inmate walking the circles had jumped another inmate and bitten her ear clean off, the biter had only been sent to sit on the very benches they now sat on until dinner.

Feeling their fear, the looming shape of the attendant entered the room like she was drawn to it. Every spine straightened against the bench . . . but Neddie's.

Edwina, who never spoke, signaled to Neddie to pay attention, and Ragno pounced.

"Stop! Stop that home signing. Now!"

Edwina was not allowed to use any hand signals that hadn't been taught by the school. It was a strict rule—all the rules at the institution were strict, and there was nothing Ragno loved more than strictly enforcing them—and she continued to berate Edwina, the torrent of ugly words coming fast. Edwina cringed, burying her hand in her skirt, and Rose squirmed against Maxine.

Maxine again pressed her thigh up against her sister's, knowing that any movement might catch the attendant's eye, and whatever horror was in store for Edwina might become theirs, so she had to stop Rose from crumbling.

Ragno drew in a breath, and Maxine hoped it was over. It wasn't.

"Speak!" Ragno howled into Edwina's clenched face.

Rose placed her hand on her heart and began to tap. Four times. Four times. Four times.

"There's nothing wrong with you. Absolutely nothing wrong with you!"

The woman was having a second wind. "Do you hear me, girl?"

No one ever used their names here. You were either "girl," if they were angry with you, or "dear," if they weren't.

"If it was up to me, I'd throw you in the back with the others. You don't belong out here. I'd toss you—"

Maxine stopped listening as she felt warmth

seeping along her thigh and, after another moment, wetting her entire underside. She quickly scooted as close to her sister as she could, caring less about movement and more about containing the situation. But a heartbeat later Dottie, who sat on the other side of Rose, leaped from the bench, the edge of her skirt soaked through, and Rose's sobs were quickly eclipsed by the tirade of furious yet gleeful cries from Ragno.

Maxine bowed her head under the weight of Ragno's rage, clasping Rose's hand in utter defeat while Rose broke down into shuddering howls as the two girls sat together in the steam of Rose's piss.

Ragno raised her hands and smacked them together three loud and distinctive times. A call for silence. The sound of the three claps was so ingrained in the girls that even Rose stopped sobbing and allowed the release of only a few snuffling sounds mixed with high-pitched sorrowful squeaks that she couldn't control. Ragno stood over the girls like a statue, triumphant.

"It is time for periodic excusing and bed," she announced. "Everyone may line up but you two." Her eyes fell on Maxine and Rose, not that there was anyone in the room who didn't know exactly who she meant.

The girls lined up against the wall, no one looking back at the two left on the bench. Not even Alice. Especially not Alice. But Ragno wasn't done.

"The two of you will sit in that piss until it's cold. And if you move at all while I take these girls to do their business like humans, you shall sit in that piss all night long."

The woman glared at them, waiting for a reaction. Maxine gave her none. This seemed to rally Rose, and only the smallest snuffling escaped her. The show of strength was too much for Ragno, who walked straight for the girls and clapped again—one, two, three times—an inch from their noses. Maxine couldn't help thinking how the claps were very much a "home sign," because this was their home. The word "home" might bring up visions of warmth and familiarity, but in its essence it really was just a word to describe the place where you lived. This was Maxine's home. It was Rose's home. It was Alice's home.

Rose collapsed onto Maxine, broken. And Ragno, satisfied, turned and led the line of girls out of the day room.

She would be back soon, and so Rose would need to stop soon, but not now.

"Did you finish peeing, Rose?" Maxine asked gently. "If you didn't, you can now. While she's gone. It's all right. It's just piss, Rose."

Maxine rubbed Rose's back like you would a child vomiting into a basin, and Rose sobbed more softly, holding on to Maxine while she released the rest of her bladder. Maxine did the same, knowing Ragno would come for them after periodic excusing, and therefore their only choice was to urinate here or in their cots. Better here, where their dresses might soak it up. Dresses they would soon change out of.

After Rose finished, she sat up, and Maxine picked the driest corner of her skirt and wiped her sister's face.

Rose balked at the gesture. "I don't want piss on me," she complained.

It was a ridiculous statement, and the two girls couldn't stop from breaking out in smiles. Rose even let out a short giggle. And then they became quiet.

Maxine's eyes flicked back to the window and the long sweeping driveway to the gate, which no longer conjured up images of country houses with tremendous hearths and a bed full of dogs. It had been a good twenty minutes since the police wagon had driven through it. If the police had been stopping at the dormitory, they would have been here by now. The girl would not be sleeping here tonight. Could home also be a small, cold, bed-less prison cell in the Back Ward? If so, then the girl was on her way home.

Maxine set her eyes on the wall across from her— as she was supposed to do, as Rose was doing—and thought about her previous home, the one sitting nine miles east from where she and her sister sat in cold piss on a hard bench. She did not have the realization that this home hadn't been very much different from the one she now occupied. Hard and cold. Instead Maxine did the thing she was absolutely best at doing: she drifted off into a dream—of visiting day at the institution, an event that happened but once a month, with the next one coming up soon. It might be the day when her mother showed up. The day she finally came for them. The day she forgave Maxine.

The day Maxine and Rose went home.

London's head throbbed where the gun butt had smacked her. The pain hadn't been helped by her head slapping the metal floor as the driver of the police wagon had sought out every bump in the road on the way back to the institution.

The wagon's brakes squeaked the vehicle to a stop. The back doors swung open. This time the cops didn't wait to see if she'd climb out on her own—not that she would have. They reached in and dragged her out by her feet. London let them. She would fight when she had to; wasting energy now was useless.

The sun was setting. How long had she been knocked out for?

They walked her roughly into the building. Not the same one she'd been brought to the day before but a bigger one, much bigger. She stumbled along between the two cops, finding it difficult to walk when she was cuffed. They were met by a nurse and two women attendants. London sized up the women, and quickly determined that this was not the time to make a run for it if the cops uncuffed her.

The cops had gone as far as they would. One of them signed a sheet of paper the nurse held in her hand, and the other removed London's cuffs and shoved her at the attendants, needing one last show of power to prove his dominance. London stumbled into the women's arms, but the cop's sentiment was lost on her as she focused her attention on her present surroundings.

Leaving the nurse at the door, the two women led London down a series of hallways. This building was darker and dirtier than the one she'd been in the night before with the girls. It also smelled worse. London had lived in enough tenements to be overly familiar with the stench. Piss and shit. The walls were yellowing, many of the bulbs were out in the hallway lamps, and although there was no actual garbage strewn in their path like inside the tenements, the floor was both gritty and sticky at the same time. The group passed rooms that looked uninhabitable, but from the coughs, moans, and shuffling sounds emanating from them, it was clear that they had occupants.

The attendants never spoke—to her or to each other. She respected them for being good at their jobs, but at the same time understood that it was a bad sign. People good at their jobs when their job was to guard you was not good news. She'd have to wait at least until their shift was over and hope for less attentive, and weaker, guards. She knew it wouldn't take long. In London's fourteen years, she'd learned a few things, and one of them was that not many people were good at their jobs.

She'd also been locked up before. Plenty of times. And that was surely where these two were hauling her, somewhere to be locked up.

Her stomach growled, and she wondered if the bread was still rolled up in her sleeve. The smell of the hallway didn't bother her stomach in the least. Nothing much ever did. The morning in the gutter, yes, but that had been another matter altogether. A matter London ignored in this moment.

She thought about what she had seen so far. A front door with a nurse's station, where it looked like an attendant also might be posted. Large windows, unfortunately with bars. Many open rooms, perhaps with windows, and perhaps with bars. The building itself had at least two floors above the one she was on, and a basement, which she was being dragged down to. She hated basements.

The stairs seemed centered in the building, and once down them, the attendants yanked her to the right. More rooms, but these doors were all closed with no light shining out from under them. Maybe offices?

London's head throbbed. She'd been unconscious when they'd thrown her into the truck. Jesus, Mary, and Henry, that old turd could have gone a little easier with the shotgun.

One of the attendants began to dig around in her uniform pocket for keys. London supposed she was close to where she'd be dumped for the night.

"I'm hungry." She might as well give it a try.

"You missed dinner," was the response from the one with the keys.

Well, that sucks, London thought, hoping again that she still had that bread. She thought about pleading the pregnancy thing, but something stopped her. She was never queasy about using circumstances to get what she wanted. Surprised by her own hesitation, she lashed out at the women.

"Ass lickers!"

No response. Not even a jerk of their arms. For the first time, London figured she might be in real trouble. What was this place? Who were these women? She'd been dragged around by someone her whole life, but as she was realizing right now, they'd all been men doing the dragging. There was something disconcerting about being dragged by women. They were more impenetrable.

The key attendant opened the door. A thick door. A door that she locked behind them. They were now in another hallway, identical to the last—long, and lined with doors—except the smell was hotter and more intense, and the hall ended in a wall. They were at the far end of the building. The only way out was back through that locked door or through a possible window in this hall.

The lighting was still dingy and dark, but it was, unfortunately, light enough to see inside the rooms as she was yanked past. Each door had a large barred window without glass. Each room held a human form and no window. London's plan had been to break out tonight. That would not be happening.

The trio stopped in front of a door. One attendant released London's arm for the first time and fumbled for the key to the room. For a moment London thought about ripping away from the other attendant, grabbing the keys, and making a run for it. But the keychain held about fifty keys, and though London had tried to watch which one the attendant had chosen at the last door, there had been no way to tell.

She tried again for the second-best thing after freedom—food. This time using what she had.

"Really, no food? I'm fucking pregnant." She immediately regretted the cuss.

The attendant unlocked the door, and London was shoved in. She hated being shoved, even if she knew she had brought this one on herself.

The door was locked behind her.

She used her new bodily freedom to race back to the barred window and shout at the retreating women.

"Whoresacks!" It wasn't truly a cuss, but in any case, she didn't regret it.

Once she heard the attendants leave, she let go

of the bars and turned to inspect her cage. It wasn't much. A room, about six by eight with a mattress. No sheets. No blankets. And London was sure the mattress was filled with piss. She bent down, picked it up with two fingers, and violently flipped it. This side didn't look or smell any better, but the physical act was something.

She went back to her door and checked out everything she could see through the barred window. The corner of a door across the hall. The cement blocks of the hallway. A piece of plaster ceiling showing the yellow stain of water damage. Not much.

The bread! Reaching down, London discovered her first bit of luck since that old mug had smacked her in the head with his gun. Pulling the bread out, she plopped onto the disgusting mattress. At least it was softer than the pissed-on floor. And she nibbled at the bread like a mouse to make it last.

Dinner at the table and two chairs on Bennington Street came to mind. The old lady was most likely about to sit down to dinner. Was it canned peas tonight? Chicken broth and bread? Remembering the salty taste of chicken broth made London ache. The stale bread could use a dip or two into that broth. She'd never tell the Missus that. How much she missed her broth.

As London licked the last crumbs from her fingers, the lights snapped out and she was plunged into a darkness so complete that she couldn't see her own hand in front of her face, not that she tried. What she did do was pull up her dirty nightclothes to use against the potent smell of the mattress, and stretch out onto it.

Because when someone locks you into a dark room, you sleep.

Rose watched the nurse lay out the instruments on the steel table: the press-on-your-tongue wood, the cold listen-to-your-heart necklace, the measuring tape. She usually enjoyed helping the nurse check her over each month—answering questions, opening her mouth really wide—but today she was too busy thinking about the girl with the dark eyes.

Rose didn't tell Maxine she'd helped the girl run. She'd wanted to tell her sister, and Alice, too, because Rose was proud that she knew about the window, proud that the girl had gotten out with her help. She loved to help. But Rose had held on to her secret, afraid that if she let it escape, the tingling feeling inside her would whoosh out right along with it.

Knowing things her sister didn't know sometimes felt nice—like stealing food, and helping the girl elope. Rose loved Maxine and loved being her little sister. But Rose couldn't help hearing the word "Mongoloid" that always sat between the other words. Often because people said it out loud that way: "Maxine's Mongoloid little sister." But when it wasn't said, when it was left out, sometimes Rose felt she heard it even more loudly.

Mongoloid.

The word made her feel like she often did while walking the endless paths of the circles. Rose had once asked Miss Barrett, one of the nice ladies who now worked in the superintendent's office, why the paths went in circles. Miss Barrett had said, "My dear, the feebleminded body is lacking a vital force. The paths circle to remove decision or choice."

Like so many things said to her here at the school, Rose didn't understand it but also vigorously disagreed with it.

Rose also didn't tell Maxine or Alice about helping the girl because she knew they'd be mad at her for doing it. Helping was dangerous. Helping meant time in the cages. But Rose didn't care. Helping felt good. Alice said this girl was the kind who would never stop eloping, and so Rose was planning to help her again.

Rose had never tried to run away from anywhere. Not even like Maxine had done when they'd lived at their other home, the one with their mother and father and brothers. Being out at night in the dark without a blanket or a bed or her stick—she shivered just thinking about it. She imagined it might feel a little like the time she got a burning-up fever and got stuck inside a bad dream where everything was all wrong and she couldn't find her way out for the longest time. When she'd woken up cold and wet and no longer in the dream, Rose had cried with joy at everything that was real.

But the girl with the long, tangled hair and black eyes, that girl liked it out there—on her own in the dark. She wasn't afraid at all. Watching her open the window had been like watching someone opening a Bit-O-Honey. The girl had been excited by the idea of climbing out the window high above the ground and out into the rainy night, so much so that she'd forgotten to look back at Rose. She'd just disappeared over the ledge.

Rose loved remembering that moment. The tickle of it pushed her to speak.

"Nurse?"

The woman's cold hands were wrapping a tape measure around Rose's head. They measured her head a lot.

"Yes, dear."

"I want to help more in the clothing room."

"Hm."

Rose could tell that the nurse wasn't exactly listening as she scribbled in a chart. Rose's measurements had filled so many charts. The numbers were like stars awakening in the night sky—a new one twinkling into sight before the last one could fully be noticed.

"I know how to fold. I'm good at folding. But you know, practice leads to improvement," Rose said, being sure to give words she'd heard them use over and over.

"Very true, young lady," the nurse said, looking at her for the first time.

Rose leaped onto this connection. "Could you ask Mrs. Vetter if I might have more practice by working the clothing room?" She tagged on a few more of their words at the last second. "I feel up to the task."

The nurse looked away, searching through her instruments. She picked up the thermometer, shook it vigorously, and stuck it into Rose's armpit. When the nurse's eyes finally made it back to Rose's, her head was tilted to the side and a sad kind of smile was on her lips. "These decisions aren't up to me, dear."

She was backing down, about to move on . . . past this, past Rose's chance. Panicking, Rose pressed her naked arm against her body, cooperating as much as possible to keep the thermometer in place. She needed to say the right thing next. But she wasn't sure what it was.

"But people listen to you," she blurted, scared she'd lost the nurse's attention.

The nurse stopped, her hand still on Rose's arm and, more important, her eyes on Rose.

Rose had done it. Following lunch the very next day, she and Maxine were given clothing room duty.

"Why are we here instead of the laundry?" Maxine grumbled.

She wasn't really asking Rose this question, she

was just complaining, so Rose didn't answer. Of course Rose knew the answer, making this another thing Rose knew that Maxine didn't. Although, this secret didn't tingle in her stomach as the last secret had. This one felt more like a sharp jab.

"It's not hot like the laundry," Rose said.

She was right. The laundry room was the sweatiest place in the whole world, especially in summer. But it wasn't summer. It was getting closer to winter, and the clothing room was a little cold since the school never turned on the gas until almost Thanksgiving. Soon it would be really cold. Winter was not a good time to elope. If Rose was going to help the girl, she had to do it soon.

"What are you thinking about, Rose?" Maxine asked, looking at her for the first time since Miss Sweeney had let them into the clothing room.

"Winter," she answered, which was true. But it wasn't the entire truth, and Rose felt another one of those jabs.

"What about winter?"

"Will you try to sing alone at Christmas again?" Rose asked.

"Audition for a solo? I don't know," Maxine said, folding another summer dress. The uniforms the girls wore came in two varieties, winter dresses and summer dresses. The first were made of a wool and cotton blend, heavier on the wool, which made them itchy, and stink a bit. The summer version was muslin, soft and comfortable. Rose hated when they switched to winter dresses, which they'd done just yesterday with the advent of November. When the girls walked the circles on a warm fall afternoon, the body odor mixed in with the wool and smelled as bad as the toilet room.

"But maybe I will, Rosy," Maxine said, smiling. "Maybe this year I'll get it."

This made Rose's heart happy. She liked that her sister was always trying for things, but she really liked that now Maxine would start thinking about singing while she folded the hundreds of dresses, underwear, socks, and towels that sat in large bins in front of them. She needed her sister lost in her daydreams so that Rose might focus on one bin in particular, the one filled with outside clothes.

Outside clothes were worn by the girls with families who visited them each month. On family visiting days, as well as on community visiting days, when the people who lived in town came, the girls who owned these special clothes were allowed to choose what they'd like to wear. Rose noticed it was the same with the boys. Although she rarely saw boys. They lived on the other side of the school and in other buildings. Girls and boys only came together for Christmas and Easter. On these holidays, when the community and families were invited, Rose would marvel at all the colorful clothes. It was like the difference, she thought, between the green trees of summer and the vivid leaves of fall. Outside clothes had soft sashes, satin bows, lace trims. They were bright blue, and deep red, and the crispest white, like the low puffy clouds of summer.

Maxine and Rose didn't own any outside clothes. Neither did Alice. Neddie did, and each month on visiting day when she put on an outside dress with a long lace collar that draped over her shoulders, the waist cinched by a thick satin ribbon, the skirt billowing around her as she walked, she looked like a beautiful princess. Sometimes, if Miss Sweeney was the attendant, she'd iron Neddie's hair so that her bangs curled perfectly right over her eyebrows and her long tresses ran down her back in ripples. Neddie would perch on one of the soft couches, surrounded by her family in the visiting room, looking like a painting. Rose couldn't help wondering what she herself might look like dressed like this, her long hair let loose from its tight braids.

"You better stop dreaming about Christmas and start thinking about folding some of those towels, Rose."

"You're always dreaming," Rose shot back.

"The difference here, Rosy," her sister said, clearly annoyed, "is that I can dream and work at the same time."

She was right. Rose said nothing and picked a stiff, clean towel up from the towel bin.

"Why don't you go fold the outside clothes, Rose. I know how much you like reading. You'll have to read all the collars and be sure to match them correctly to the cubby names. Can you do that?"

Rose nodded at Maxine—she didn't trust herself to even smile, afraid she'd whoop with joy at her great luck. Rose moved quickly over to the colorful bin, and her hands shook as she picked up the first dress, a blue gingham with a tight-looking collar. She checked the name. Lucy Mitchell. After carefully folding the dress, she scooped it gently up onto her palms as if it were the crown of a queen, and walked it over to the wall of cubbies, where she stood reading all the names neatly printed on labels, until she found the right one. Triumphant, she slid the pretty blue dress into the cubby and tapped the dress four times . . . lightly, so as not to dent her work.

"Nice job," Maxine said, rolling her eyes. "Now do that about fifty more times in the next thirty minutes, please." But she laughed. And Rose laughed too. Loudly.

If Maxine had been paying attention—which she wasn't—she might have noticed how much of Rose's laughter came from nervousness, as Rose had been one heartbeat away from stealing that dress. She had been so very close to rolling that blue gingham up into a tight ball and shoving it under her skirt. But she hadn't. Thank goodness. Because stealing a summer dress was pretty silly. The girl would need a warm dress, of course.

Rose folded another. And another. She folded alongside Maxine until her stomach growled and her back ached. Though she folded what felt like a hundred dresses, the bins never seemed to empty. While she worked, she thought about the nickels. Clams and a sandbar. That's what you needed to run away and stay away. It's what all the girls said. Rose couldn't trade Neddie all her apples for a sandbar, but she could trade them for nickels. Neddie gave Rose a nickel for every apple. She'd collect some clams for the girl with the black hair . . . and also an outside dress. Rose didn't like the thought of the girl running in the darkness in just her nightclothes. Rose didn't like the thought of being out in the dark at all, but to be out in the dark in her nightclothes scared her even more.

Now she heard Maxine's stomach growl. The whistle for dinner would blow soon. She needed to steal a dress. Fast. Rose couldn't be sure she'd ever be in here like this again.

When Maxine bent way down into the bin to pull out the last remaining towels, Rose made her move. She had been folding a brown woolen dress. It looked like it might be a little large for the girl, but better this than too small. Rose hated tight clothes. She rolled the dress quickly sideways and then stuffed it under her skirt, half into her underwear. Then she plucked up the next dress and began to fold. Maxine's head popped back out of the bin, her arms full of towels.

"I wish Alice could be in here with us," Rose said, a little breathless.

Maxine stopped for a minute and gazed at the wall, smiling the special smile she used whenever she thought about Alice. "Yeah," she said. "They barely ever let her out of that mangle room, except maybe to sew."

The next dress now folded, Rose needed to walk to the cubbies and place it in. It was Dottie's, and Dottie's cubby looked really far away.

"Alice is good at the mangle, though," Rose said.

Maxine leaned down again into the bin for more towels, and Rose made her move toward the cubbies, hoping that the brown dress was tucked securely enough not to drop out of her skirt and onto the floor. It didn't.

"But Alice is good at a lot of things, just like me," Rose said. Which was true.

Maxine stopped folding and smiled broadly at her sister. "I love you, Rosy. You know that?"

"I know that," Rose said. She could see the sadness in her sister's eyes. It was because tomorrow was visiting day. Maxine always got sad right before visiting day. When it was a while away, Maxine could still imagine that their mother was coming. But as the day drew closer, it grew harder for Maxine to hope.

Their mother was never coming. But Rose would never tell her big sister this.

Maxine sighed, and then turned around and bent over her folding table. Rose immediately hiked up her skirt and shoved the entire stolen dress inside her underwear, so that it could not slip, no matter what. She adjusted her skirt over the top of the stolen dress so that it didn't poof out all funny-like, and then walked back over to her bin and pulled out another dress.

The key entered the lock.

Maxine turned around and surveyed all they'd done, and then looked at her sister. "Not too bad," she said.

Rose agreed.

She felt a little bad, but *not too bad*.

London heard the door unlocking at the end of the hall. She kept her eyes closed. This was her second morning in this room, and yet she was still so tired. She'd slept through the first night like a rock, only to be woken up by an attendant with water and hot oatmeal, which she'd devoured, and then she had fallen asleep again for the rest of the day. They'd not come back until evening—with soup and bread and milk, which London had promptly eaten, and then she had fallen into another deep sleep. She'd woken in what she believed was the middle of the night when she'd heard someone crying, but she'd turned over, and before she knew it, she was listening to the key in the hall door and sensing the lights on overhead.

Stretching, she slowly opened her eyes. They were going room to room, unlocking doors and giving out breakfast. The smell of oatmeal floated through her barred window. Her stomach growled. She thought about the baby in there, wanting food. She hated mawkish thoughts, and never had them. She rolled to a sitting position on her mattress, brushed the hair out of her eyes, and waited for her breakfast.

A face appeared in London's window. They were checking to be sure she wasn't hiding in wait for them. Satisfied she wasn't a threat, the key slipped into the door's lock. London wasn't foolish enough to jump someone when there was a hallway full of food and a morning full of people. But she understood the drill.

An attendant in a gray uniform opened the door, while another came in with a tray. London didn't move from her mattress. The last thing she wanted was for this woman to spill any of that oatmeal onto the sticky piss-soaked floor.

The woman, older, with graying hair pinned up under her cap, smiled at her. London didn't smile back.

The woman set the tray down, but London didn't move for it. Though she was starving, she would wait until these two passed on before she ate. It was a weakness to dive in, and London wouldn't show any weakness. She'd let that oatmeal turn to cold paste before she touched the spoon.

"You okay?" asked the woman.

London stared at her. She couldn't tell why this woman had asked this. Most likely to see London break down, cry, beg to be allowed out. Although, truthfully, London felt pretty good. Two days of sleeping and eating had really been what she needed. She decided to answer honestly, test out this place. But before she could, the woman spoke.

"I've spent some time here," she said. "So has Maddy." She gestured at the other attendant outside the door by the cart of trays. Maddy didn't respond.

"You work here now?" London asked.

"We live here. And work here. You'll work today too. They'll be in for you after breakfast."

London nodded. This was good to know.

"Let's hurry, ladies." The booming voice came from out in the hall, probably one of the women who'd dragged London down into this place.

"Enjoy your breakfast," the gray-haired woman said.

As soon as the door was shut and locked, London did just that.

They came for her about twenty minutes after breakfast. First they made her pick up her piss pot and carry it to the toilet, dump it, rinse it, and return it to her room. After which they herded about twenty women from the tiny rooms into a large shower, where the attendants made them undress and had them bathe. The water was freezing but felt glorious, especially on London's bruised face. London had heard about warm baths or showers, although she'd never in her life had one and so didn't wish for one now. The thought of dunking herself into water as warm as tea seemed like a dream. The old lady liked to say that wishing was for boobs. London always liked this about her. Here in the showers, deep within the basement of the building, the air was warm, and London washed her hair, something she rarely ever did. As the cold water ran down her back, she even allowed herself to miss the old woman, a little.

They were each given clean underwear, socks, boots, and a stiff woolen dress. London braided her long, wet hair, letting the water naturally squeeze out as she twisted. She was beginning to think that being hit with that man's gun wasn't the worst thing in the world. A few days of rest. Some hot food. A shower. None of it was bad, and it fortified her for another jump out of this place. Because no matter how good it felt to be clean, she wasn't about to stay locked up. This time she'd keep moving until she got home.

They were led out of the showers in a line and up the stairs, escorted by attendants, and not the kind in the drab gray dresses who had brought breakfast that morning. These women had more substantial uniforms, and more substantial arms and faces. London wasn't going to run right now anyway. Not while she was being watched. She'd wait until they released her back into the dormitory with the other girls, which she was sure they would eventually do. She would behave and be released, and then take off like a jackrabbit.

The group in the line ranged in age from those younger than London to women almost as old as

Thelma Dumas. A few of them looked pretty ragged, even after the shower they'd just had. Others seemed empty, like the horde of workers leaving the Bremen Street railyard at the end of a long shift. A few were rotten apples. London could pick them out of any crowd. Crappy people. They were everywhere.

Every door the group approached needed to be unlocked and was then locked again behind them. And there were a lot of doors.

It was brighter upstairs, with real sunshine streaming in through the windows, which raised London's spirits even more. The bits of blue sky she could see made her itch to be out there, running. Even the air, still fragrant with piss and shit, was at least tinged with vinegar, like they'd attempted to clean.

The line of girls and women turned down yet another hallway. The next door opened up onto a large room, and before they were allowed in, the attendant at the head of the line called out, "Enter and take a seat on the bench."

London smelled the room ten paces before she saw it. Her stomach rolled, and her heart beat fast. Fear. It was an uncomfortable sensation that she despised, and she coughed it back, along with the vomit rising into her throat. She straightened herself up, daring whatever was in that room to come at her.

Women. Women were in the room. Women everywhere. Lying on the floor. Naked. Clothed. Rocking.

Wandering. Humming. Dancing. Moaning. All around her. Like a slow, shuffling nightmare. Through the fog of it, London heard the attendant bark at the line of them to sit, and she slid onto the bench, her knees buckling under her. She leaned back and tried to breathe, the stench pressing in on her, thick, warm, and horrible.

The room was large and open, with windows to match its size. But the morning light seemed to stop at the glass, as if it weren't strong enough to penetrate this place. Benches lined the room like at a railway station. The attendants began handing out buckets and rags, and the women from the tiny rooms began to work, scooping up the shit, wiping up the piss, from the floors, the benches. London felt her heart start up as the attendant came closer. It wasn't shit scooping that scared her but staying in this room . . . all day. She couldn't stay in this room.

There were only three of them left on the benches. The attendant said something and motioned for them to follow. London didn't know what the woman had said. She just knew that somehow she was getting the chance to leave this place, and she rose to her feet, tripping on the heels of the girl ahead of her.

Several unlocked and relocked doors later, they were in a large shower, much like the one London had used an hour earlier. She and the other two girls were told to stand on one side, and each was handed a hose. Somewhere, someone turned the hoses on, and

London had to grab hers with both hands to keep it from whipping away as the water burst from it. The girl to her right laughed at London's surprise, and London almost turned the hose on her . . . but the idea of being returned to that room stopped her.

A door opened, and in stumbled women, naked women. One, two, three—up to six. They lined up against the back wall of the shower, hunched and moaning from exposure. The girl who had laughed took aim and squirted the women closest to her in their torsos. The women shrieked and turned away, making for the door, trying to protect themselves from the cold, hard water. They had to know before they reached the door that it would be locked. Everything was locked here. There was no way out.

"Let's go," snapped the attendant, who took a seat on an old wooden chair in the corner of the shower room.

The girl to London's left aimed her hose at the women nearest her. London noticed how she started at the women's feet, slowly allowing them to get used to the water before she raised it higher. London glanced at her. A white girl with dark red hair, most likely Irish, most likely Southie. London followed her lead, hosing the women from the feet up.

The women cried and curled into protective stances, except for one. She just stood. She didn't move or turn or flinch, the cold water making dents in her skin wherever it hit.

"This is shitty of us," London growled.

The girl from Southie glanced over at her. "Shitty world."

"How long you in for?" London asked.

Now the girl took a long look at London.

"What?" London asked.

"You mean, in therapeutic confinement?" she asked.

"No, in this place. This . . . hospital, or whatever it is?"

"The Fernald School," the girl said. "I'm here for life. Just like you. Just like all of us."

"For life?"

"Segregation of the unfit," the girl said, and shrugged. "You have been deemed unfit. This isn't prison. There is no parole. You just live here now, like me . . . like them." She motioned with her chin to the women in front of them.

Receiving bad news was not a new experience for London. Her entire life was a series of people giving her bad news. "Your father is dead." "Your mother is dead." "The orphanage is full." "The foster family doesn't want you." "The gas has been shut off." "There is no food." No, there had never been any shortage of bad news. Still, this little nugget lodged itself up underneath her rib cage while she took it in, making her breathing shallow—like she'd been punched in the stomach. Probably she was out of practice since living with the old lady, along with the other thing.

"And my baby?"

London had never said it out loud before. Her baby. She couldn't imagine it yet, what it actually meant—having a child. Though it was becoming harder to ignore. Because any bad news she received, it also received.

The girl didn't look at her then.

More bad news.

"You been diagnosed an imbecile or a moron, right?" she asked.

London didn't answer. She had this strange urge to add the words "high-grade" to the word, like the nurse had done. But she wouldn't use their words to make herself sound better.

"I'm a moron," the girl said, choking out a laugh. She looked over at London then, and London saw that it had hurt her to say the word. "They say it's hereditary. What we have. That means we will always have it."

"And my baby? What happens to it?"

"It stays too," whispered the girl. "Forever."

The attendant clapped her hands hard. The girl knew the signal and sprayed the women right in their heads, the clapping being some sort of sign to wash the women's hair. The women hunched and twisted, shrieking anew. One of them shit, dark and long, onto the shower floor.

"Animals," whispered the attendant.

London turned and sprayed the attendant directly

in the face. She sprayed her for a solid two minutes before she was jumped from behind and dragged from the shower room.

For five days London scooped shit into a bucket in the Back Ward.

Alice stood on the choir dais next to Maxine. Choir practice was almost always a restful hour—for all of them—as taking direction and working in a group came easily to those whose entire lives depended on these skills. Although, this morning even the peaceful tones of "O Holy Night" being gently sung on repeat didn't seem to be settling her.

A few days before, she had watched Rose hide the dress deeply in the heating grate behind her stick. Alice had wondered if she should tell Maxine but had decided not to—because tomorrow was visiting day, a bad day for Maxine. The monthly cycle leading to visiting day was like their menses, the heaviest flow being the day before, the day of, and the day after. The day before was when Maxine's hope that her family would arrive was dying . . . yet mercilessly not dead. The day of was the death of this hope. A day spent surrounded by the happy chatting families of others roaming the campus, their arms loaded with presents and packages. The day after—dark silence, before Maxine could rekindle her dream . . . which she always did.

Also, everyone was entitled to her own secrets. Alice had hers. Why shouldn't Rose have a few? Alice did wonder what she wanted with the dress, but not for very long. Most likely, Rose just wanted to steal.

Except for Alice and Mary, all the girls stole all the time, and not because they cared about Miss Sweeney's red scarf or the pen in the nurse's station— they didn't, and often Alice noticed that the girls ended up tossing whatever it was they'd stolen, into a bush along the path to the gymnasium or into one of the cafeteria trash bins. It was what they did here . . . steal, scribble, slap, smash. All of it helped to break the endless routine of the whistles, the circles, the periodic excusing, the clapping to stand and dress and undress, the poking and prodding of thermometers and needles and measuring tapes, the charting of their every move while being on display for visitor after visitor after visitor, and the endless hours of feeding bedsheets into the hungry jaws of the mangle machine.

But when Alice went into the grate to retrieve Rose's stick for her and discovered the neatly stacked nickels and pennies hidden even farther back in the duct, she was concerned.

Stealing was fine. And Rose was good at it. Alice had watched her liberate plenty of rolls at dinner—that girl loved her bread—and Alice had always been impressed with Rose's abilities. She was thoughtful about the person who was standing nearby, quick and decisive in the moment, and even faster at throwing everyone off balance with her toothy smile. Alice was confident that Rose wouldn't get caught. But stockpiling money and clothes, that was different. Rose's strange thefts seemed to highlight the uneasy feeling Alice had been having lately that things were changing.

For Alice, there was always the worry of their ages. Every day she and Maxine crept closer to their fifteenth birthdays, Maxine's in September, her own sometime in October. In less than a year, they would both graduate from the girls' dormitory to the women's dormitory . . . only two hundred yards across the institution's grounds, but an entirely new world. Having been given every lowly job that existed inside these buildings, Alice had seen most of this world, and there was cause for concern. The first being Rose.

Even if the school ignored the fact that Rose was a year younger than Maxine and allowed her to come with them, the three of them could still be separated inside the large women's building, where though they might be in one another's sights, they might spend little, if any, time together. Worse, one of them might be sent out to a farm. Mostly it was the men who were sent out to the farm cottages miles away, to grow food for the inmates here at the institution, but women sometimes went too, and they never returned.

Living on a farm didn't scare Alice, but living without Maxine did.

Alice loved Maxine. She loved all Maxine's dreaming . . . about living in mansions, being a famous singer, seeing the ocean, even her excruciating visiting-day dreams where she was sure her mother was coming. She loved how excited Maxine became when they had liver for dinner. She loved the way Maxine was able to smile through so many things. Her grin, just like Rose's, seemed to open up her entire face. She loved Maxine's crooked teeth, especially the one in the front with the chip out of it. She loved how hard it was for her to get out of bed in the morning, and how her hair always had a knot in the back of it, and her goofy laugh that sounded like a small dog barking. She loved her lips. She loved her smell. Alice loved all of her . . . in the very way she wasn't supposed to. This was Alice's secret.

Alice felt no shame in loving Maxine. None. Though unashamed of her love, she *was* afraid of it— that someone might find out, or, worse, Maxine might find out. The first would send Alice to the Back Ward forever, and the second, well, Alice didn't want to think about it. Too many things could go wrong. Things she had no protection against. Fortunately, the first lesson Alice had learned at Fernald was that though the girls might be constantly observed, no one ever saw anything. Alice's secret was safe. Locked away deep inside where no one could ever get to it. Not any of the doctors, nurses, teachers, attendants, and visitors who crawled over the institution like ants, watching them, always watching them. They could stare at Alice every minute of the day until she took her last breath, but they'd never catch a whiff of her most precious possession, her only possession.

But they could take Maxine away. They could send her to a farm. Or worse, they could lock her up for all her dreaming . . . deep inside the massive brick building where the girl with the wild look in her eyes was spending her days. Where every girl who'd ever tried to run was put to work. The Back Ward.

Alice had seen a large portion of the institution . . . except for the boys' dormitories, where girls were never allowed. She'd seen the Sick Ward filled with a sadness as thick as Bessie's arms, and she'd spent time inside the dreaded therapeutic chambers called "the cages." But they were nothing compared to the Back Ward, where not a single visitor had ever stepped foot. It was a place much worse than the Sick Ward, where at least there was a way out, through either health or death. The Back Ward was a place where the body just continued to exist. Endlessly.

The music stopped.

"Alice? Was it you who hit that wrong note?"

Miss Petruskavich stared up at her, and Alice tensed, though she could see it in the woman's eyes that she was teasing. Miss Petruskavich loved to tease.

"I was listening, Miss Pet," Rose called out. "She hit every note."

"Thank you, Rose," the woman said, putting her hands together like she was praying, and tipping her head to Rose. It was a gesture their music teacher did often. And it removed the woman's eyes and attention from Alice.

But Alice remained tense. Nice white people could be more dangerous than mean ones.

Alice never sang, a fact that both Rose and the music teacher knew. She only mouthed the words, which she had forgotten to do today. Miss Pet, as they all called her, didn't mind Alice's partial participation. All Miss Pet ever asked was that the girls in her choir allow her to play and sing, and to share music with them. And, of course, that when they stood in front of the community, or visitors, or Dr. Greene—the balding superintendent of the school—they sing . . . or at least pretend to.

Choir was well attended. Even Edwina was in choir.

Now that November had arrived, choir practice happened two times a week instead of once a month, as Christmas was on its way. The institution accepted visitors year-round and allowed the community in on visiting days for small concerts and poetry readings, but Christmas was the most widely attended event. Alice couldn't have cared less about Christmas, poetry, the community, or singing, but like all the girls, she enjoyed listening to Miss Pet pound her keys and belt her tunes. It was a place where no one ever caused trouble. Not even Bessie and Ellen.

"Sopranos, please take over."

Alice could now stand without pretending to sing—she and Maxine were altos—and she immediately returned to worrying, but was interrupted by the opening of the chapel door.

Everyone's eyes but Miss Pet's moved to the door. In walked the girl from the police wagon, followed by Mrs. Vetter, the head nurse, a small but substantial woman with short yellow hair and a sharp gaze.

The first thing Alice noticed was that Rose had stopped singing. The second was that the girl was carrying a book. None of this made sense, and Alice liked for things to make sense.

Miss Pet smiled at the visitors and continued leading the sopranos to the end of the piece, giving her guests time to make their way to the piano.

Alice—along with every other member of the choir—kept her eyes on the girl as she traveled up the middle aisle. The girl was not limping. She didn't hang her head. She didn't look sick, or even any skinnier. All signs that she'd survived the seven days inside the cages better than most. She also kept herself behind the nurse by half a step. She was learning.

As the two approached the group, the girl never looked up at the wooden choir dais, but Alice could tell she was seeing them all, taking the entire scene in through her skin. Alice didn't need to look at her long to know that this one wasn't nearly done fighting this place.

A conversation ensued between the two women. It continued on for a bit; Miss Petruskavich was a lover of words just as much as a lover of music. The choir shifted and swayed, losing interest in the happenings down below.

"She's been gone a long time," Rose whispered.

"She survived fine," Alice said.

Maxine glanced her way. She was checking Alice out, trying to peek inside her. Alice wouldn't let her.

London sat with them at dinner. Rose invited her. This was the girl's name. London. How odd to be named after a city somewhere far away. All Alice knew about the city of London was that it had a large building with a clock on its side. She'd seen a picture of it once. Her education was seriously lacking, even if she had been living at a "school" for the bulk of her life. Although she'd always been a willing student, her classes at the Fernald School consisted mostly of resoling shoes and mending clothes. She must have cobbled an army's worth of boots and let down the hems of the skirts of every female inmate at Fernald, along with many hems for the children of the nurses and doctors, whose clothes somehow made it to the school's worktables. The only one in the whole institution who could out-sew her was Helen.

Alice understood how the world of Fernald worked, but she didn't know much about the world outside anymore except that this girl somehow still smelled like it, a mixture of chilly spring air and gasoline.

"Were you in the cages?" Rose asked.

Rose obsessed over the cages because it was a place without Maxine. A place where you were alone.

"They're called therapeutic confinement chambers," London said, never raising her head from her soup bowl.

Alice exchanged a look with Maxine.

"And besides the mattress smelling like piss, it wasn't that bad. The food was the same as we're eating now, and I got a lot of sleep."

Alice didn't like anyone to intrude on Maxine and Rose and herself—it wasn't part of the "keep your head down and do your work" way in which she lived—but she had to admit that this girl's answer to Rose was kind, even if the girl had a roughness to her that scared Alice.

"You gonna eat that?" London pointed at Maxine's bread.

Maxine slid the bread closer to herself.

The girl with the city for a name ate on.

"Your cheek is better. It had a big bruise. Remember?" Rose said.

"Look at this," the girl said, putting down her spoon and lifting up her mop of hair to reveal a large gash on her forehead. "A gift from the wrinkly bumhole who turned me in."

Rose let out a little gasp.

"We're not allowed to cuss," Maxine explained.

"You're shitting me," said the girl, stuffing half her bread into her mouth and not for a second understanding what she'd just done.

"Aren't you going to eat your apple?" Maxine asked Rose, attempting to change the subject.

"Not right now," Rose answered, tapping her apple four times and looking off into the dining room.

Rose was lying.

Alice shifted on her bench but said nothing.

"Saving it for later, huh," said the girl. "I never do that. Someone could swipe it from you. But they can't steal it if it's in your gullet."

"I'm saving it for later," Rose said, echoing the girl.

Another lie.

Rose didn't usually lie, and she never lied to Maxine. Alice held her breath, waiting for Rose to say something . . . else. To explain why she wasn't telling the truth. To explain the apple, and the dress, and the money slowly adding up in the vent.

Instead Rose chatted away to the girl.

"Why is your name 'London' and not 'Betty' or 'Dorothy' or something?" Rose asked.

"Don't know," the girl said. But Alice could see that she did.

"Where'd you get that book?" Rose asked London.

"*The Count of Monte Cristo*." Maxine read the book's spine.

"The yellow-haired nurse gave it to me," London replied.

"Why?" asked Rose.

The girl shrugged.

Again Alice could see that London did know, but this time Alice wished she'd answer. It was curious that Mrs. Vetter would give the girl a book. And such an important-looking book, with its deep-red cover and the title in silver lettering that you would be able to feel if you ran your fingers over it.

"Can you read?"

London looked up at Alice in surprise. Alice was a little surprised too, and it took her a second to know that she'd actually spoken that out loud.

"Yes."

It looked like the girl wanted to add something more, but didn't. Instead she kept eating, ladling the soup from the bowl to her lips in short, loud trips.

Alice could read, but not very well, certainly not well enough to read a book like that. She'd been a high-grade moron when she'd first tested at Fernald, but her latest test had showed that she'd slipped to a low-grade. Alice despised the names, and the tests. But the truth was, she could feel herself slipping, unlearning things she'd once known. Stitching hems and washing bedsheets didn't help you learn. Mrs. Vetter would never have handed her a book.

"Where's your sandbar?" Rose asked next.

"That means 'Where are you from?'" Maxine explained.

"Eastie."

"By the airplane field?" Maxine asked.

Alice was annoyed that the girl had said something to interest Maxine.

The girl nodded.

"Have you ever seen an airplane take off? From the ground, I mean, and not just fly overhead. Our math teacher, Mr. Ragno, he's been up in one."

Maxine was now facing the girl on the bench, even leaning in toward her like she wanted to be closer to her next words. Although, the only thing that fell from the girl's mouth was soup, dripping down her chin. The girl ate like she was starving, lifting the bowl and sucking down the dregs of soup, and then wiping her face with her sleeve. A soupy sleeve that Alice would be washing tomorrow, along with a thousand other soupy sleeves.

"Sure I have," she finally said. "Jeffrey Field isn't far from where I live. They make a big deal when they take off. But I'd never go up in one of those rickety heaps of shit."

No one bothered reminding the girl of the swearing rule.

"I'd go up in one. In fact, I am going up. One day," Maxine told her.

"I doubt it," London said. "Some Irish bim at the hoses says you never get out of here."

"What are the hoses?" Rose asked.

London chugged her milk instead of answering.

Maxine stiffened, startled by the reality of London's response. This was why Alice didn't like anyone around them. They all knew Maxine was never going to fly in an airplane. Maxine knew it too. She was also never going to be a singer, or see the ocean. Or get married. Or have children. Or do a lot of things. But no one had to say this out loud. There was nothing wrong with a little dreaming. Nothing.

The girl slammed her empty glass onto the table. "Unless you bust out of here. You could always bust out of here."

"Yes," Rose said, "unless you run away, Maxxie. Then you can fly in an airplane. There's a map in the hallway outside Mrs. Vetter's office, and the airplane field is right on it. Miss Barrett showed me the pictures of all the tiny planes. You could run away and climb onto the first airplane you see."

Alice watched London stop eating for the first time since they'd sat down. She was obviously taking in the information about the map. Alice noted with satisfaction that this girl was planning another elopement. The sooner the better. Alice had enough to worry about.

"Thinking of running, are you, Rosy?" Maxine joked.

Alice choked on her soup.

"Are you okay, Alice?" asked Maxine.

Alice shook her head.

"She doesn't talk much, does she?" London said.

"Sure, she does," Maxine said, defending her. "When she feels like it. Which just isn't that often."

Alice warmed with joy at Maxine's defense of her. If they had been allowed to touch, Alice would have pressed her knee up against Maxine's in thanks. Although, just thinking about this made Alice glad that she couldn't.

London picked up her bread. "I get it," she said.

Alice saw that she did get it. But this still didn't mean Alice wanted the girl to stick around.

That night was a Miss Sweeney night. So Alice lay with her head at the bottom of her bed and let Maxine rub her bad foot. She rarely thought about her foot, though it ached all the time. On the nights when Miss Sweeney watched over them, Maxine would rub away at the pain until Alice drifted off to sleep. Sometimes, when it got dark, Alice would let the tears slide out of her eyes the entire time Maxine's warm hands kneaded the knots from her sole, until her thin pillow was soaked through.

Before lights-out, Alice noticed that Neddie had an apple. She knew it must be Rose's. Rose often stole fruit and gave it away to Lizzie or Sarah or anyone who looked like she'd had a bad day. This, along with the absurdity of the idea that Rose was collecting money and clothes to elope, made Alice feel better. Rose would never run.

Maxine's hands kneaded, kneaded . . . and slowly, with each squeeze of her fingers around Alice's tired foot, everything began to feel better. There was the problem of their birthdays. But this was an old worry, and one she had time to figure out. There remained that one small niggle, deep in Alice's belly. Rose's lie.

Maxine kept rubbing, and soon . . . that niggle rubbed right out.

London had lived in a lot of lousy places, and even she had to admit to herself that this was not even *close* to the worst of them. You were fed three times a day. There was a mattress . . . pissed on or not, it was still better than the floor. In the dormitory there were even blankets. And she'd been given a book! She'd never been given shit before, not even by the old lady. Although, it was because of the old lady that London had been given the book.

After a week inside what the girls here called the cages, she'd been brought to the head lady. London had met her kind before. Smarter than most of the people around her and more than a little frosted about it because she'd never get the respect that the two tie-wearing knobheads did who sat in the larger offices on either side of her. Women like Mrs. Vetter were tough to chisel. London was sure she'd have been back in the cages if it weren't for the book.

It had been sitting on the desk. London had first noticed it because it was bright red, but then couldn't take her eyes off the name on the cover. Dumas. Like the old lady's name. The nurse, seeing London's interest, had asked if she could read.

London had given her the truth. "I love to read."

Mrs. Vetter was shocked by her answer, and London saw instantly how charmed the nurse was by her honesty. The woman shocked London back by plucking the book from her desk and offering it to her, telling her she could borrow it for as long as she liked. At the same time, Mrs. Vetter informed London that she would be returning to the dormitory.

London was thrilled, and she gingerly accepted the book from the nurse's hand.

It was heavy, and the cloth covering it was soft and an even brighter red when it was held close. London turned it on its side to read the name again, Dumas, and found that it was written in silver, and not white like it had looked when the book had been sitting on the desk. She ran her finger along that name, feeling the letters under the tips of her fingers. And then she looked up at the nurse in earnest and placed the book back on her desk.

"They'll take it from me. The attendants. I can't have it."

Mrs. Vetter stood so abruptly from her desk that her chair scraped the hard floor.

"No one will take this book from you. You can be

sure of it. The matron will be informed." She picked it back up and stretched it out to London, smiling a powerful, conspiratorial smile.

Getting a book, getting fed, sleeping off the ground, it was all good, but London couldn't forget the word the pretty Irish girl had used. "Hereditary." London didn't know its exact meaning, but she understood that whatever they said she had, it was stuck to her, and she couldn't get rid of it.

She looked over at Rose, sleeping less than a foot away from her. The girl was goddamn adorable. London had to give her that. She was all curled up and snoring lightly while she held on to her stick like it was some sort of baby doll. Rose had signaled to London before falling asleep. She'd pointed at the vent between their beds and then pointed at the window that London had climbed out of a little more than a week ago now. Obviously, there was something in the vent, and this girl was going to help London. Again.

London settled onto her cot. She hadn't planned on running right away. She wouldn't make the same mistake twice, running out into the woods, not knowing where in God's piss hole of a world she was. She needed to see the map outside Vetter's office that Rose had mentioned. She needed to know which way to run.

London twisted around on her cot. She couldn't sleep. It was way too early in the day.

"Cut the noise," someone growled from across the room. Most likely that brute with the bangs.

"Kiss my crack," London whispered, plenty loud enough for the brute to hear.

Maxine's head popped up from behind Rose's sleeping face, and Alice's head from behind Maxine's. They both stared her down.

London stared back. She understood they were trying to help her, but she didn't need their help. Although, she might need Rose's. She turned her back to them . . . loudly, daring that brute to say another word. She didn't.

Although, now London lay there in a lather. She should just break open that vent tonight after all these mollies fell asleep. Keeping out of trouble wasn't something London did well, and she knew it. Maybe she'd beat the sausage out of that bitch tomorrow, get it over with, and be sent back to pick up shit for another week. That wouldn't be so bad. She reached for her book and pulled it close to her, just like Rose had done with her stick. They'd take the book away from her for sure.

She'd let the banged bitch keep her face arranged the way it was, for now. She'd hang out with Rose, and Maxine, and Alice. She'd be patient.

Maxine was all right. A little loopy. London didn't agree with making wishes about shit like flying in airplanes. It got you thinking that things might be different, and that life wasn't crap. London wasn't sure yet about the black girl. Alice. She knew Alice didn't like her because she thought London was trouble. She guessed Alice was right about that. The girl was protective of Maxine and Rose. London had to hand it to her, she'd chosen two hard ducks to protect, a Mongoloid and her gooseberry sister. Anyway, it didn't look like Alice had much of a choice—London could easily see that the girl was in love with the gooseberry.

Falling in love was crap.

London allowed herself to be swept into the routine of the institution. Waking before the sun. Sitting on the toilet for thirty minutes. Dressing. Walking. Eating. Working. She got to know which attendants left the longest butts in the ashtrays. How to secure seconds at meals by getting in the front of the line, and then having Sarah or Neddie watch her first plate while she reentered the line for a second. And to be especially sweet to the kitchen staff so she'd be placed on dish duty each afternoon instead of laundry, because the laundry room was as hot as hell. All the while she carried her book wherever she went, and no one said a word. Although that dora with the bangs made eyes at it now and then, and every time she did, London floated it out toward her . . . just a teensy bit, with the lightest of *Go ahead* thoughts, because London itched to jump that bitch.

The girl's blue-eyed ghostly pal never looked London's way. She was obviously the smarter of the two mugs.

London's favorite part of the day, other than reading for an hour on the benches before shitting and bed, was walking the circles. She liked the endless looping paths that brought her round and round, where she could walk and look out over the changing fields and trees. The leaves were gone now, and the sky had that stone-gray look of winter, but without the terrible bite of cold yet. The empty branches of the trees stood out, dark against the sky, like fingers running their tips through the low-hanging clouds. And the smell. London could honestly say that the earth was the nicest thing she'd ever smelled. She didn't know what it was. . . . The dirt? The dying leaves? The bark of the trees? Or maybe it was the spitting rain that often fell while they were out walking so early in the morning. Whatever it was, she sucked it right in up to her eyebrows, making her . . . something. Happy, she guessed.

It was one of these mornings, walking the circles, when she thought she felt it for the first time.

She wasn't sure. It could have been gas. The old lady had always complained of pains in her stomach. "Acid," she'd say, all doubled over until it finally loosened up and came out. She was a noisy farter, Thelma Dumas. She was probably farting right this minute. Sitting in her chair and passing loud gas as she howled out the window at some poor boob. God, London missed that farting bitch.

She'd take her back, Thelma would. And the baby, too. She had to. London might or might not be a moron . . . like this place said. But she knew her baby wasn't a moron. She wouldn't let it be.

At that moment she reached for it, but then Rose skipped up next to her, and London dropped her hand quickly to her side.

"Hey," London said in greeting. This one was growing on her like one of the barnacles lining the piles of the Clyde Street Pier.

Rose looked around, the smile on her face never changing, and she then leaned in toward London. "I've been stealing stuff for you," she whispered. "Clams. A whole bunch of them."

London had been waiting for this. She already knew what was behind the grate. A mounting pile of nickels, dimes, and pennies . . . and a dress. Of course she'd stayed up that first night and checked it out while everyone was asleep, and had continued to check on it any night when she couldn't sleep, which was most nights. She knew Rose was gathering things to help her run, and this time successfully. But more than money and clothes, London needed to see the map. She couldn't just run off into the woods and hope to find her way back to East Boston.

"Thanks for the help," London said. And she meant it. "But no more stealing for me, okay?"

"But I like helping you," Rose said.

"Then go see that map," London told her. "The one with the airplanes on it. That would really help me. Ask that lady you like if she'll show you the roads to the airplanes. And then remember them and tell me."

"I'm great at remembering things," Rose said. "Probably I'm the best person at remembering things you ever met."

Rose had swagger, and London liked a tomato with a little swagger. "Can you remember last Christmas?"

"Of course," Rose said. "That's easy. We had a big dinner. With lots of biscuits. I love biscuits. And then we went to church for a long time of singing. The boys came. And visiting-day people."

"Visiting-day people?" London asked.

"Yes," Rose said. "A lot of people."

"That's the day I'll run. Christmas." It was about a month away, which would give her time to finish reading the book, and she still shouldn't be showing by then. "What do you think?" she asked Rose.

"Run after the dinner," Rose said. "Because of the biscuits."

London laughed. "You know, Rose, you're pretty smart."

"I'm an idiot."

Now they both laughed. Loudly.

Miss Sweeney called out, "Come now, dears. Quiet down."

London looked up and noticed Alice watching her. She and Maxine were walking together across the circle. Maxine had gotten used to London and Rose hanging out. Maxine had even come to like London a bit, reminding her about the cussing whenever the attendants were nearby. But London knew Maxine would like anyone who was kind to Rose. Alice, though, still didn't trust London. In London's experience, black folks didn't trust white folks easily, and for good reason. London wasn't white like Maxine and Rose, but she wasn't a Negro, like Alice and Mary. She was a dago. The word was nasty, but for London it brought to mind the smell of her father's hair, and the feel of her arms wrapped around his neck.

"Tomorrow is Thanksgiving dinner," Rose reminded her. "They let us have seconds on turkey."

"I've never had Thanksgiving dinner before," London admitted. Sometimes she found herself telling Rose things she'd never told anyone else. She didn't know why.

Rose grabbed her hand. "You can have my seconds tomorrow. That will be thirds."

London snatched her hand away. "We can't touch, remember, Rose? That's a rule."

"But you never follow the rules."

London saw that she'd hurt Rose.

"I don't mind breaking rules that get me in trouble. But I don't break rules that get you in trouble. Do you understand?"

Rose's eyebrows bunched together. "I understand stuff."

"Rose, don't be mad, okay. I didn't mean it like that."

"But you said it like that."

"No," London said. "I didn't. I just wanted you to know that . . ."

"What?"

"That . . . I like you. And I don't want anything to happen to you."

Rose's smile was bright and large, and it startled London every time she saw it.

"I like you too." Rose beamed. "We're friends. Right?"

London smiled. "Okay."

"Say it. We're friends."

"Rose!"

"Say it."

London really couldn't understand how this puny monster was about to force her into saying they were friends. Though, she knew it was true. The realization had hit London a couple of days before, on her way to dinner, when Rose had asked London to tell her what was happening with the Count of Monte Cristo in her book, and London had said she would once they'd gotten their plates. And then London hadn't been able to wait while Rose took all the time in the world on the food line and making her way to the table. That girl did not move fast under any circumstances. London had watched her slowly walking past table after table, saying hi, and "Excuse me," and smiling at people, and London was like, *That bitch better hurry it up* . . . because she wanted to be with her. And now here London was, about to say something she'd never said before in her life.

"We're friends."

"Ha!" Rose laughed. "I knew we were. Even if you couldn't say it. I knew it."

"Goodness, dears. Morning walks are for our constitutions, not our mouths," Miss Sweeney complained, frowning as she passed.

London had a friend. Her very first.

If she didn't count Alby, that fuck.

Maxine had gotten it into her head once again that she would like to be a singer. This year she also added the goal to learn the piano. In Maxine's mind, all singers needed to play the piano, because Miss Petruskavich sang and played the piano. Maxine ignored the facts that Dottie sang rather prettily and didn't play the piano, and that Mary played the piano and didn't sing. The Christmas concert always featured a solo or two, and Maxine had finally secured one.

Since London had arrived at the school, Maxine had more time to think about things like singing. Rose had been spending much of her time with London, walking the circles, sitting with her at meals. London was even reading that book to Rose, the one with the silver writing on its spine. Maxine and Alice would listen to a chapter or two now and then. It seemed to be all about escape and revenge—a little strange of

Mrs. Vetter to give this story to a girl who seemed overly obsessed with both these things. Maybe the nurse had never read it. Maybe she'd just had it lined up on her shelf with other books, as a sort of display. So much about the institution was display—the large brick buildings with their massive columns, the well-tended walkways, the deep and comfortable couches in the family visiting room. Couches Maxine had never sat on. Until, maybe . . . Christmas.

Maxine had convinced herself that her entire family would arrive at Christmas. She and Rose would be fifteen and fourteen this coming year. She would be an adult. And besides being able to take on full-time work, she'd be a tremendous help with her brothers. It made sense for their mother to wait until Christmas to bring them home. With the entire school and community present and her family sitting among them, Maxine would come to the piano and sing. The homecoming would be triumphant. Hope flooded Maxine's heart.

When they'd first arrived at the school, Maxine's heart had been flooded with righteous anger. How dare her mother send them away! Maxine had done nothing. Or, at least, barely anything. Also, she and Rose had never given their mother a moment of distress. They'd always looked after themselves, allowing their mother to concentrate solely on their younger brothers.

But over time, that day in the alley had begun to weigh on Maxine. It grew larger, and her feelings more intense, and she doubted her innocence. How could she be innocent when even then she had admitted she was wrong? She walked the circles morning and afternoon, begging her mother in her heart to forgive her. She could change. Anyone could change. It had been a mistake. Her heart was so broken, she was sure her mother could feel it all the way in Somerville. How could she not? How could she not know how desperately sorry Maxine was . . . and come for them?

But she never did.

It was then that Maxine had turned to her last resort: God.

At night, after Rose fell asleep, Maxine prayed. Both her parents had been pious, church-loving people, and Maxine knew many good prayers by heart. But being so tired from the long days in the institution, she'd fall deeply asleep before she'd even finished saying "Dear Lord."

But she worked at it. Maxine loved to work hard. She might not catch on quickly to things, like Alice, but she saw that over time, if she put in the effort, she became better, and in this way she grew into quite the devoted worshipper. Her bad thoughts, the terrible aching, that day in the alley . . . each night she stripped herself bare before the Almighty. Yet in spite of cracking open her heart, Maxine and Rose remained at the school.

If Maxine had been laid low before, she now slipped even further into despair. She had never been a great thinker, but she searched her mind for reasons why this could be happening. Using the very few years she'd had to observe the world in all its wonder, she hadn't been able to come up with an answer. In a state of pure unhappiness in the face of an uncertain future, she had reached out to the aging Dr. Fernald.

Surprisingly, the superintendent of the school had granted Maxine an interview. She was sure he would wipe away the sadness and confusion she felt upon being exiled from her home, for this was the man who ran the large institution she and Rose now existed in. The very person who decided when the whistles blew, how many claps of the hands meant quiet, what the inmates ate, when they slept, and even the times when it was correct to move one's bowels. Not only did he manage all of this, and more. . . . He also constantly tested and measured them, and therefore certainly understood the contents of their hearts and minds.

Maxine sat across from the doctor in his office as she waited for him to finish reading her file, which he read straight through in front of her as she patiently swung her feet to and fro underneath the wooden chair. She felt sure this grandfatherly old man with a thick mustache and thinning hair would have the answers she was looking for. After she sat listening to the ticking of the office clock and watching the dust float in the sunshine streaming through the office window, he removed his glasses to look across his wide desk down at Maxine.

"Dear child," he began, and Maxine felt the confusion and sorrow already lifting. "You have committed no crime."

Maxine's mind reentered the alley, as it had done so many times before, and like so many times before, she felt shame. It was as if she and the doctor now both stood there, in that glorious moment that had turned so terribly wrong. Maxine felt immediately weakened. Vulnerable. She stared into the watery eyes of the old man and waited for him to forgive her.

"It is lucky that your mother recognized your feeblemindedness at an early age, before you could acquire the facility to commit crime. Because, my dear, every moron, especially the higher-grade moron, such as yourself, is a potential criminal, needing only the proper environment and opportunity for the development and expression of his criminal tendencies."

"I'm a her," Maxine had whispered.

"I don't believe you're understanding me," he said, returning his glasses to his face. It was a sign that he was finished. Although, he had one last thing to say, and he said it without looking at the withering child in the chair, whose boots were now still.

"The moron is a most dangerous element to the community. From a biological standpoint she is an inferior human being. It may sound harsh, but it is scientifically objective." He seemed to emphasize the "she" as a gift to Maxine.

She'd climbed down from the chair and calmly left

his office, and naturally, rage had taken over. Pure. Complete. Rage. Maxine had burned with it, day in and day out. There was Rose to think about—which Maxine did, and therefore she locked her intense anger inside, where no one could see it, like the deep, fine punctures she made in her fingertips using needles stolen from the sewing room. The hate she felt could only be satiated by slowly shoving the tiny slivers of metal through the pink of her flesh—physical pain masking the emotional, a beautifully welcome trade-off. And afterward, Maxine would drift off into blessed sleep.

In this way, from the tiniest annoyances like the constant lack of toilet paper to the very real physical dangers from the bigger girls whose anger whipped outward instead of inward, Maxine quenched her fury by sinking needle after needle into her fingers.

She'd thought about killing herself. Thought about all the ways in which it could be done, some less nasty than others. But there was always Rose. Maxine was stuck, and without hope. The only peace being the pain of the needles.

It was Alice who'd saved her. *A beautiful love story*, that's how Maxine thought of it.

One night, in the dark dormitory, with everyone asleep, Alice had reached across the six wide inches from her cot to Maxine's—their eyes locked on to each other's—and had gently taken the needle from Maxine's finger and plunged it into her own.

There had not been the faintest twitch of Alice's beautiful lips, nor a tinge of pain in her deep-set steady eyes. But to say that there was nothing would be wrong. It would be very wrong. Because there was absolutely something. There was connection. One so raw and real that Maxine vowed in that moment to love Alice forever.

After this, Maxine's hope returned, and though the hoping hurt so much worse than any needle ever could, she didn't care. She was in love with Alice.

Of course, she'd loved Rose all her life, and Rose had been the one to keep Maxine from death, but Alice was another kind of love, a love that made Maxine want to live, to once again imagine her mother forgiving her, and coming for her, and for Rose. This love made Maxine want to get a job and find a home, close to the ocean. Where she and Alice could hear the waves. It made Maxine want to dream of old houses to paint and nice furniture to arrange, soft furniture, like that found in the visiting room. Alice was a love that made Maxine want to plan a life.

It was like she'd lived through a long fever, and now she saw life the way it really was. All the dreaming would pay off one day. All the hoping. Maxine now had no doubt. Alice didn't see it this way, but that was fine. Maxine understood. Alice wasn't ready yet, and so Maxine dreamed for the both of them.

Singing. Playing the piano. It was all part of the plan. Christmas was the best day for her mother to come. Christmas was special everywhere, but especially here at the institution. It was still early December, but the lights were already strung across the fronts of the buildings, and red and green tinsel was hung inside the main rooms and offices. There was even Christmas music in the dining hall playing on an old phonograph placed in the corner by the door. Everyone chewed as quietly as possible to hear it, even London. There was change in the air. Maxine could smell it. She could also hear it, since all she did was sing, sing, sing.

Miss Pet was caught up instantly in Maxine's enthusiasm. She arranged to meet with Maxine at special times before or after choir practice. Maxine was an attentive student. She was also a terrible singer, a fact that bothered neither student nor teacher, and together they decided on "Deck the Halls" as Maxine's debut as a soloist. Miss Pet believed it a perfect fit for Maxine's voice. Miss Pet would invite the entire school and community to join in behind Maxine with the "Fa la la la las," and Maxine's performance would be the great finale to the evening.

Maxine turned out to be a much better pianist than she was a singer, and Miss Pet gave her exercises to practice between their sessions. Maxine wasn't allowed more time at the actual piano, so her teacher showed her how to strengthen her fingers when she was away from the instrument.

"Place your hand on the table as though you were resting your fingers on the keys," she instructed, closing the piano and showing Maxine on the lid. "Now play the sequence one-three-five-two-four, repeating it over and over."

Maxine gave it a try.

"Make sure you keep to a rhythm and that each note you play is given equal pressure." She showed Maxine how some of her fingers were stronger than the others, and how she shouldn't favor those but make sure her weaker fingers did their share.

"It's easy to allow one, three, and five to carry the weight for you. Don't. Make that two and four work."

Maxine practiced everywhere: at the table during meals, on her thighs as she walked the circles, while she and Rose folded clothes and towels, even during periodic excusing, where she stood in front of the sinks, playing on the porcelain. Sometimes Maxine thought she could actually hear the music in her head as she played.

Over time, she graduated from one-three-five-two-four to the actual notes of "Twinkle, Twinkle, Little Star," and then to "Deck the Halls," and even to Tchaikovsky's *Swan Lake*.

Sitting in the day room on Christmas Eve, Alice gave Maxine a "Pst."

Maxine quit playing and looked up. The matron was passing.

"Don't let her see you doing that."

"Why? The concert's tomorrow. I need to practice my piano."

"That's just it. There is no piano."

"There is in my mind."

Alice sighed. "That's worse."

Maxine would have loved to tell Alice not to worry so much. But Maxine would never tell Alice not to worry—worry was what held her together. Instead Maxine moved her fingers only in her head, like all ten of them sat inside her brain, and the only things that actually moved were her thoughts.

"Stop," Alice said.

Maxine smiled at the wall across from her, being careful not to turn to Alice. Mrs. Ragno was on duty tonight, and Ragno was always on the lookout for special feelings of friendship she could use against the girls. "Are you inside my head as well?" Maxine said.

"As well as what?" Alice asked.

Ragno clapped her hands four times, saving Maxine from answering Alice's question. It was time for periodic excusing.

Since Ragno locked them in, the girls were free to roam about the bathroom for the twenty or so minutes before they changed for bed. Maxine happily took her place in front of one of the only sinks that wasn't broken, and began to practice.

"Move," Bessie said.

Maxine moved on to the next sink in the long line of sinks. It was cracked, but it would do. She started from the top.

"Move," Bessie said, shoving Maxine away from the second sink.

"This one doesn't even work." Maxine was so

caught up in her practicing, she didn't realize she was challenging Bessie.

Bessie realized it, and she grabbed a fistful of Maxine's hair and dragged her over to the working sink, and shoved her head under a cold stream of water.

Sputtering for breath, Maxine caught sight of Alice standing up from the toilet, and reacted. She ripped her head from Bessie's grip, leaving a large clump of hair tangled in the girl's fingers.

"You—you can have all the sinks, Bessie," Maxine sputtered, with the intense sincerity that comes from fear. She had to stop this before anything else happened. Before Alice made another move. Any girl could be punished here, horribly punished, but Alice and Mary were especially vulnerable.

London stepped between Maxine and Bessie, and Maxine knew she was losing control of the situation. She looked around for the only person who had the power to stop this now. Ellen. Who sat quietly on a toilet, smiling and watching with interest. This was about to explode.

"Bessie," Maxine said, trying to get around London—who wouldn't allow it—though Maxine knew all was lost even before she heard London's next words.

"Come at me, bitch."

Before Bessie could react, Rose leaped at London and hugged her tightly around the arms, shouting, "NO, NO, NO, NO, NO!"

Maxine was in shock. All she could do was watch as London struggled to free herself from Rose while

Bessie attacked, pelting London directly in the face, knocking both Rose and London into the sinks, and then onto the tiled floor.

Rose scrambled to her feet ahead of London, and now Maxine leaped in between Bessie and Rose. "Bessie," Maxine tried. "Bessie, please."

This had to stop. It was Christmas tomorrow. The day when she'd sing for the entire institution. The entire community. Her mother.

"I have nickels," Rose shouted from behind Maxine. "I'll give you nickels."

Ellen gave a cough, and Bessie reacted by dropping her fists to her sides . . . but not unclenching them.

London was now back on her feet, but Edwina, Dottie, and Helen had ahold of her. Between the three girls, and Bessie's well-placed punch, which had landed hard, London was wrestling to clear her head and stand straight.

The lock in the door turned.

The girls froze, except for Edwina, who let go of London's arm and stepped in front of her.

Ragno clapped.

The girls reacted, marching toward the door. Mary pulled out a bundle of toilet paper that had been hidden up her sleeve, and quickly wiped the blood from London's face as best she could.

"Oh, you little scavenger," Bessie hissed over her shoulder. "You're gonna pay for hiding that paper."

London went for her, but Rose was again in her way.

"Please," Rose whispered. "Tomorrow's Christmas."

London stopped. But Maxine could tell it was taking everything the girl had to hold herself back. Maxine had never been more thankful for her little sister than she was right then. A brawl during periodic excusing would definitely excuse them all from the Christmas celebration. Maxine couldn't even imagine it.

Maxine and Alice waited until most of the girls had filed from the toilets, so that they might file out directly ahead of Rose and London. Maxine could hear London's breath coming hard and fast behind her. She willed the girl to calm down. The clothing room was even closer quarters than the toilets, and if London stormed into it, things would return to ugly.

Rose continued to whisper to London. Maxine couldn't make out exactly what she was saying, but tiny snips of it were coming her way. Something about a plan, and one night—and the disconcerting sound of Rose's pleading voice. But then Maxine heard it, the word "nickels." And she remembered Rose saying it a few minutes before, in the middle of the terrible scene. She had nickels. What nickels?

The clothing room was silent as the girls changed. This was normal with Ragno on duty, and therefore Ragno was unaware of the tension as the girls pulled their arms out of dresses and yanked nightclothes over their heads. Maxine stood close to Rose, trying to catch her eye, trying to understand what was happening. She felt as unsteady as London had looked after being socked by Bessie. She couldn't find the right places inside her head for any of the words or actions that were going on with her little sister. Rose . . . whom she'd slept next to every night of her life, whose air she'd been sharing since before she could remember, who felt like part of her own body . . . now felt distant, though she stood an inch away.

Maxine could also feel Alice, undressing on the other side of her, understanding this strange moment. Kneeling down to remove her boots, Maxine tried to catch Alice's eye, but Alice refused to look back, concentrating on her own laces.

The jumpy excitement that had been racing through Maxine's body a half hour before was replaced by heavy dread. What was happening? How had it all gone from Maxine happily practicing on the sinks—something she'd been doing every night for a month—to her clunkily changing into her nightclothes next to Alice and Rose and not knowing them at all? Why did Rose have money? Why wouldn't Alice look at her?

A series of claps had them filing out of the room, down the hall, and entering their dormitory bedroom. Maxine walked without feeling her feet, or the floor. . . . It was as if she were walking directly into a dream. A bad dream.

The girls climbed onto their cots. Maxine didn't attempt to communicate with Rose, because she was now sure she was in some sort of nightmare, and you could never do what you wanted in a nightmare.

Numb, her mind spinning, Maxine couldn't feel the parts of her body that were touching Rose.

Ragno stood at the door as she always did, finger on the light switch, waiting, as usual, to signal to the girls lined up on their beds that she was in control, and would shut it off at her leisure, not theirs.

Maxine didn't want it to go off. She didn't want to be plunged further into darkness. For the first time in her life, she didn't want Ragno to step from the room. But then she got her wish.

"Mrs. Ragno," came a voice, one not often heard, especially not ringing out for all to hear.

"Yes, Ellen?" Ragno said, removing her hand from the switch. Even this woman could tell that if Ellen was speaking out, something interesting was about to happen.

No one moved. Maxine stopped breathing altogether.

"I'm sorry I have to report this," Ellen said, not sounding sorry in the least. Maxine could see the girl sitting up on her cot. "But it seems that Rose has stolen money."

Maxine flew from her cot. "That's a lie!" she screeched.

Ragno clapped her hands three times, which did nothing to shut Maxine up.

"Liar!" she screamed at the top of her lungs, over and over, with all the pent-up uncertainty that had been building since the sinks. She felt Rose's arms pulling at her, trying to stop her. But it was useless.

Maxine shrieked and shrieked until Ragno slapped her across the face.

The matron now rushed in, along with two women attendants from the other sleeping rooms on the floor. None of the girls moved from their cots, and even Rose shrank back onto hers at the sight of so much authority.

"What is the meaning of this?" asked the matron calmly.

"The Mongoloid stole money," Ellen said, pointing at Rose. "It's probably in the grate with her stick."

"Stick?" the matron said, confused. Ragno was already at the grate, yanking it open.

"I did it," said Maxine desperately. "I stole the money."

"No!" Rose moaned. "No, no, no." She rolled into a ball on her cot, hiding her face.

"There's also a dress in here," Ragno said from where she knelt on the floor.

"I stole that, too. I stole the dress. And the money. I was going to elope. I had a plan. To use the nickels, all the nickels," rambled Maxine, trying to employ as many of the words she'd heard Rose whisper. "It was me. I hate this place. I hate this place, and I hate all of you."

Rose began to sob, but Maxine couldn't stop herself. Not now. All the hopelessness she'd tried to shove aside for all the years she'd been here opened up and swallowed her. "Do you hear me? I hate you! I hate you! I hate you all!"

She didn't look at Alice. But she knew Alice understood, which made the pain even worse. It was like Maxine had lost her sister and the love of her life and her chance to play the piano and sing, and her mother.

Her mother was never going to come. Her mother was never going to forgive her.

They dragged Maxine across the room, along with the dress and the money. She bit and tore and dashed herself furiously against the women who held her, not knowing up from down or their bodies from her own. They threw her to the floor. Her cheekbone—still throbbing from Ragno's hard slap—was driven into the wood planks while they shoved her arms through the cloth of the jacket, and her shoulders strained awkwardly as they bound her. After flipping her around, they tied her ankles. Her only freedom was her voice, until that was gagged. The last thing Maxine saw as she was dragged from the room was Alice.

Reaching to the floor to retrieve Rose's stick.

London lay on her cot staring up at the peeling plaster ceiling, waiting for Bessie and Ellen to jump her. She was more than ready.

The thought had occurred to her to jump them first, and that thought had included a lot of pummeling and blood. Especially as she'd lain listening to Rose's sobbing, which was just now finally beginning to subside. Bessie would be easy. London had known so many Bessies. But that ghost bitch was another matter. London had come across pure evil in her life only a few times. Working it over did nothing. You needed to stay the hell out of its way. And now London had put both Maxine and Rose directly in its path. She needed to leave. Tonight.

As the hours passed, London began to realize that those two soft potatoes weren't coming. A move on her tonight was more Bessie's style. Someone like Ellen would have bigger plans. So now London lay awake waiting for the right time to flee.

Out of the corner of her eye, she could see the cot next to her. It was empty. Rose had climbed in with Alice and was now wrapped around the girl, clutching her stick. Though London told herself she didn't care that Rose had chosen to be comforted by Alice over her, she did. *This is the reason why you don't make any goddamn friends,* she told herself.

The image of the old lady sitting at her window floated before London's eyes. She was the only one who understood that the world was a place filled with two kinds of people, crappy people and crappier people. At the moment, London felt she fit more in the latter pile, which soothed her dark heart just fine.

She needed to move her mind to more pressing matters. Like the fact that she now had no money and no clothes. And that she'd have to jump the fifteen feet to the ground, since the steam was definitely coming through the pipe tonight. The thought of jumping pleased her. She'd never been afraid of heights and was actually in the mood to drop hard to the ground.

At least this time she knew which way to run. Thanks to Rose. Rose's friend Miss Barrett had helped Rose find her way to the airport on the map. She had only been able to remember the first road. Trapelo. Rose said that to find Trapelo the lady had moved her finger past the gymnasium on the map, and then past the administration building. Once on Trapelo Road, Rose said, the lady had moved her finger down, which meant London needed to make a right. After this, Rose said, the lady's finger had gotten lost in all the roads, and even the lady had had trouble, and they'd given up and just admired the airplanes.

It didn't matter. All London needed was that first road. That first direction. This was the way out . . . the way home. The roads where the lady's finger had gotten lost were obviously in Boston.

After a while Rose stopped whimpering and fell asleep. London could hear her wheezing breaths, cut short by high-pitched hiccups left over from her crying. Alice was also asleep, although London could tell she had lain awake a long time.

Still . . . she waited. She wasn't taking off until the darkest part of the night, right before the edges of the world began to brighten. She'd found people slept soundest closest to the time when they needed to wake. When she finally crept out of her cot, she could just make out the dark forms of all the sleeping bodies.

She stared over at Ellen, half expecting to see the girl's sinister-assed eyes staring back at her. But she was asleep. London watched her body rise and fall with each breath. The idea crossed her mind to walk over to the cot and smother the bitch to death. But London absolutely knew she wouldn't. If she was going to kill Ellen, she wanted that molly wide awake for it.

London looked down at the book in her hand, and then over at Rose. Before she could change her mind, she slipped the book under Rose's pillow. A gift, she guessed. Or maybe an apology. She didn't know. She'd never offered either one before. Then she tucked her blanket under her arm and made for the window.

It opened easily, and she tossed out the blanket, climbed out onto the stone ledge, closed the window as best she could so that the cold air wouldn't wake anyone earlier than the whistle, and jumped.

The fall wasn't nothing. She smacked the cold ground hard and rolled onto her back, her legs zinging from the impact. But the blood was pumping, hot and fast through her body, and she sprang up, retrieved her blanket, and took off across the lawn, keeping to the trees.

After creeping past both the gymnasium and the towering administrative building, she dashed into the dark like a rabbit, and quickly came upon the first road that wasn't part of the school, where she turned "down," just as Rose had said.

Striking out, she stuck to the woods a few feet off the road to keep from meeting any early morning risers. They'd know exactly where she'd come from, being shoeless, wearing nightclothes, and being covered in a blanket. She wasn't cold, not even her feet. Not yet. The excitement of being out alone in the night kept her warm. But she'd need shoes and clothes soon. First, though, she needed a place to hide, the closer to the institution the better, because they'd be looking for her farther out. Not in such a tight circle surrounding the grounds. She was going to be smarter this time. Take her time. Think.

London picked her way through the woods alongside what had to be Trapelo Road. There were a few farmhouses, but she hurried past them. She wasn't doing that again. It was almost dawn. If she had to, she would retreat into the woods and cover herself with leaves for the day, although she sure hoped she wouldn't have to. Except for her feet, she was pretty clean. If she was lucky enough to find clothes and shoes, and braided up her hair, she might actually be able to walk along the street during the day. But once she spent a night under a pile of leaves, it would be harder to look like any other girl on an errand for her mother.

Coming over a hill, she caught sight of a small neighborhood. It was farther off her road than she would have liked, and in the wrong direction, but London didn't have a choice. She turned toward it, and after a minute began to run, needing to beat the lightening winter sky.

She arrived at the collection of brick and wooden structures. She spotted an empty-looking three-story brick building and headed for it.

She broke through the back fence easily and entered a yard full of tall grass growing up through the slats of old crates. She tried the back door, then the basement window. Locked. Using the corner of her blanket to wipe off a small circle of dirt, she peeked in. She couldn't see much, but she could tell no one was moving about inside. She grabbed the largest empty crate she could find and dragged it over to the window. After looking up at the building, and then around at the houses on either side, she wrapped her hand inside her blanket and punched in the window by the lock, opened it, and climbed inside, pulling the empty crate in front of the hole she'd just made.

It was definitely warmer. And dusty. Filled with old milk bottles and tools that London didn't recognize. She investigated the entire floor, looked out all the windows she was able to reach, and tried the door. It was locked.

She quietly collected a few boxes of bottles and built a small wall in front of the window she'd broken, to protect herself if someone walked in the door while she slept, and then she settled down. She was asleep in a matter of seconds.

When she woke, she peered out the tiny smudge of window she'd cleaned earlier in the morning and guessed it was mid-afternoon. She felt rested, like she'd slept for a while, although a little stiff, and her feet were cold.

It was quiet. Eerily quiet. She figured she was in some sort of small factory or store and wondered where everyone was. But then she remembered. It was Christmas. She almost laughed out loud. No one would be looking for her, or at least no one would be looking for her very hard.

Christmas.

She couldn't stop herself from thinking of Rose and her biscuits.

She stood up to dispel the memory, flapping her arms and legs about to warm up. She walked about for a bit, found a nice corner to pee in, and then wrapped back up in her blanket and dozed off again. Tonight she'd be back on the road. But for now she'd stay right where she was.

As soon as it grew dark, London opened her window and crept back out into the tiny yard. Picking her way over the clumps of grass and old crates, she looked through the slats of the fence into the yards on either side of her, seeking food, clothes, shoes. She wasn't hopeful, and for good reason. There was nothing.

She could use the blanket as a coat, or as shoes . . . not both. She chose the coat, and then squeezed out of the fence the way she'd come in.

London knew she could do without food for a few days, but she needed shoes and clothes to keep going. She didn't want to take the risk of wandering about in this neighborhood, but she had no choice. Also, anything she stole might be reported, and then they'd have an idea of where she was, so it was better to steal here than along Trapelo Road, where they'd know her direction.

Keeping close to the buildings, she made her way to the street. No one was out. But she could hear the clinking of glass, talking, and laughter inside some of the houses as she snuck past. Christmas dinner. Her stomach growled. She might not need food, but she certainly would have liked it. She pictured Rose sitting in the dining hall among the lights and tinsel. She hoped Rose was eating. She didn't picture Maxine.

London spotted a house with no lights on. Carefully she circled the house, checking out every window she could reach, and listening. There was no sound.

Hunched as low as possible, she crawled up the stairs onto the back porch. And there, sitting by the door, was a pair of old boots! She snatched them up and took off.

London walked the rest of the night, her feet flopping about inside the boots, the blanket wrapped tightly around her. The houses were clustering more thickly now, and London looked about for hanging laundry, but of course no one left laundry out overnight. As she passed one house, she heard faint singing, and stopped to listen. The "Fa la la la las" of Maxine's song were unmistakable. She hurried on.

How long would they keep Maxine in the cages? London tried not to imagine her, bucket in hand, cleaning the shit from the floor in the Back Ward. Instead she hoped Maxine had passed a quiet day in "therapeutic solitude."

London's feet began to drag. She needed another place to hide soon, and to sleep. Spotting an abandoned-looking shed standing all on its own close to the road, London crept inside through a large hole in the bricks. It wasn't the safest place to hide out the day, but she was exhausted. Again she fell asleep without one thought crossing her mind.

She was woken up well before the sun rose, by a pounding rainstorm.

After stretching, peeing, and then curling back up in her corner, she slept another hour or so, but then couldn't sleep anymore. London lay sprawled in the dirt listening to the rain. She was cold and hungry, and worse, she missed Rose. For the first time, she wondered if she should have run.

But if she'd stayed, Rose might never have spoken to her again. She was sure Maxine never would. London was sure Maxine had already figured out that Rose had stolen the money and the dress for London— and was sure Maxine believed that London had put Rose up to it.

As the rain battered the roof of the shed, London relived the horrible scene. The scuffle at the sinks. Bessie's punishing kiss between the eyes. That evil bitch calling out from her cot. And then London remembered Alice sitting bolt upright in her bed.

Alice had known about the money and the dress.

Maxine's terrible screeching, the attendants piling on top of her, the strength of the girl's emotion as they shoved her into the straitjacket. All that hate, spewing from her like vomit. It had been directed at Alice. London saw it clearly now. Maxine didn't blame London. Maxine blamed Alice.

London twisted onto her side in the dirt. She'd long ago given up being surprised at the shitty ways in which life often worked out. Wondering why was a loser's game she never played. She reached for her book and then had to laugh. Like Rose's stick was for Rose, the book had become something of a comfort to London. She had finished the book twice. She would have read it again. And again. It was about a man who was wronged by his friends and sent to prison for life, and when in prison he makes a new friend, then breaks out, finds a treasure, and exacts slow and painful revenge on those who wronged him. A happy story. Even though it had the old lady's name on it, Thelma would have said it was a piece of crap. Because there never is any escape. Definitely never a treasure. But . . . there can be revenge.

London went over the last few weeks in her mind . . . singing in the choir, reading her book to Rose, sleeping in a warm bed. Could she have stayed? Could she have lived there?

She thought again of the old lady and her opinions.

No. London wanted to go home, because that dump on Bennington, it was where she belonged. She and her baby.

Her baby.

London had seen enough squawkers to last her a lifetime, but her very own? She couldn't imagine it. Although, a kind of warmth was beginning to settle in next to the fear.

The old woman would take her. Both of them. She had to.

London unwrapped herself and stood up, stamping her feet to wake them. It was still raining. She checked the road in both directions to be sure she was alone, and then wandered about the broken-down building, opening the drawers of a dusty workbench, poking into corners, and rummaging through crates. Nothing. Or at least nothing useful. There were chains, old ropes, splintered barrels, a cart without its wheels, and then . . . hanging on a hook and looking very much like a ripped curtain . . . a pair of work overalls.

London yanked them down, shaking out any bugs and dust. They were big, and as dirty as hell, but they were clothes. She kicked off her boots and pulled on the overalls. The legs of the pants were much longer than hers, and she needed to stuff the ends into the boots. The extra fabric allowed the boots to fit more snugly and warmed her feet at the same time. She still looked like a runaway, but at least she wasn't in nightclothes anymore.

London used the rest of the time before it became dark to turn over every board in the place so as not to miss out on a shirt or coat, but finding nothing else, she got on her way.

The gloomy day had passed into a dark evening, and it was a long night of walking. By the time the sun was hinting at rising, she was entering Cambridge, her blisters screaming, and she found herself gloriously surrounded by an awakening city. She was no longer a runaway but a regular ragamuffin walking among the growing crowd.

London walked through Cambridge, over the Harvard Bridge, and into Boston in a dreamlike state. She could hear her boots clunking and scraping along, yet they sounded far-off and detached from her. She arrived at the Court Street station in the same circumstances in which she'd traveled the entire trip— penniless, and so found a doorway stoop in an alley, to rest and think. She slept on and off for the rest of the day with the comforting hubbub of automobiles and people streaming up and down Tremont Street. Slipping onto a streetcar without paying would be best accomplished in a crowd, so London needed to wait until the end of the business day.

No one took notice of her. It was busy, and people had things to do. With late afternoon coming on, she spit onto the corner of the filthy blanket she'd been carrying for two days and cleaned her face, and then tossed it away, braided her hair, and headed for the station in her nightclothes and overalls.

The platform was crawling with people. She dropped her head, and when the streetcar pulled in, wiggled expertly between the exiting and entering crowds, slipping onto the car. She'd never paid for a streetcar in her life, and today was no different.

The dull lighting inside the East Boston Tunnel was strangely soothing, and London nodded off while standing on her feet. It only took a few minutes to travel beneath the harbor, but when the car pulled out of the tunnel, it was dark, and London was greeted by the gaslights of Maverick Square. She clutched the nearest hanging strap, at the sight of so much familiarity. She was just a few blocks away now. Jumping out of the institution's window, the cold nights on the road, the long walk through the city of Cambridge, the day spent in and out of sleep in the alley, even Rose and Alice and Maxine . . . it rushed away, and she leaped from the car while it was still moving.

Chelsea Street was crowded, and cold. Her feet might know exactly where they were headed, but they still complained about taking her there. Finally Bennington Street came into sight, and London began to run.

Turning the corner, she ran on, half tripping while she focused on the window slowly coming into view. Was it open? Was she there? What horrible profanity would the old lady shower down on London when she caught sight of her? Not that it mattered. Any old horrible thing would do.

London ran faster. But then she slowed. The window wasn't open, and no light shone through. London stumbled to the front door and shoved it open. She started up the sticky stairs two at a time, her breath in her ears and her blood pumping against her skull.

She tried the door. It was locked. She pounded . . . already knowing. Now she attacked it, smacking at the wood with her fists so hard that she could hear the wood splitting.

Off in the distance, behind another wall, a threatening voice rang out.

London stopped and slid to the floor. The old lady was gone. Thelma Dumas was gone.

London had no idea how long she sat there. Finally she rose to her feet and headed down the stairs. On the middle landing she spotted a large hunk of the umbrella stand, most likely kicked into the shadowy corners of the stairwell on the day she was taken. She picked it up.

Dirty and cold, she walked out into the street. When she passed over Chelsea, she realized for the first time where she was heading. To Flannery's butcher shop.

To Alby.

He couldn't help her. He wouldn't help her. She didn't hate him for this. At least not right now. She remembered how he'd thought she was funny. How he'd laughed at the things London would say. In a good way. But she always knew Alby was limited inside—a sensitive white boy who might allow himself to fall for a dirty dago girl from the streets, but he didn't have follow-through. She just really had nowhere else to go.

The shop was closed, the windows dark and empty. Each night, Alby and his brother removed the dried and netted beef, ham, and coppa that hung in the window, and placed it in cold storage. Better not to entice hungry vagrants. Not that London was hungry. She wasn't. She wasn't anything, really, besides cold.

Around her were the sounds of East Boston: dishes, voices, automobiles, even the belligerent honking of a tugboat echoing not far off in the navy yard. She stood and listened while she watched her glowing reflection in the butcher shop's window. Then, after raising her arm in the air, she whipped the umbrella stand shard through the glass.

The hole was bigger than she'd imagined the fist-size lump of clay could make. Interestingly, the hole wasn't round but more like the shape of a star. A pretty star. She looked around for something else to throw. After loosening a cobble from the street, she picked it up and whipped it through the glass.

Another star.

Digging out as many cobbles as she could, she pummeled the shop window until there was nothing left of it. Only then did she notice the small crowd gathering around her. Some on the street. Others hanging from their windows. Everyone staring.

Exhausted, she dropped down onto the curb amid the broken glass and waited for the police wagon.

Rose woke with the whistle. Alone on her cot, memory stung her belly. Maxine was gone. This was the second terrible morning that Rose was forced to wake to this realization. It felt like someone had piled rocks on her. Lots and lots of rocks. Making it hard to breathe.

She let some tears slip out, though Alice had told her she was not allowed to cry anymore, crying time was over. The key turned in the door, and Rose quickly stuffed her stick under the mattress alongside the bar of the bed, its new hiding place next to the book. She climbed from the cot, forgetting to wipe her eyes and nose . . . and Alice saw she'd been crying.

"Rose."

Alice was scared. Alice was so scared.

Rose immediately wiped her snot and tears on her sleeve and began to make up her cot. The only thing that made Alice better was if Rose tried to do exactly what Alice had whispered to her the morning before. So many words coming out of Alice. Like water from a faucet flooding into her ear.

She'd told Rose to feel her feelings. But only on the inside. Never on the outside. She explained that Rose was like a walnut. Her feelings were the soft, tasty meat nestled inside her. They had just enough room in there to move around but not enough that they could become jostled or bruised. It was dark and warm and safe in there for the feelings. A place where the feelings were kept fresh and alive. Her body, Alice told her, was the wrinkly shell. Hard. Sealed at the seams. It kept the meat safe. Rose had to be like the walnut.

Rose didn't really understand, but she tried. She tried to be like a walnut. For Alice. And for Maxine. Rose collected all the tears she wanted to cry every time she remembered Maxxie saying she'd stolen the money. Every time she pictured her sister tied up on the floor, screaming. Every time she turned her head to find Maxine, and she wasn't there. They filled up Rose's stomach, those tears, and when she couldn't hold them inside her wrinkly shell anymore, she threw them up into the toilet, into the dirty laundry pile, anywhere that no one would notice.

During periodic excusing that first morning, she didn't play in the water but sat on the toilets for the whole thirty minutes, sometimes peeing, sometimes pooping, and sometimes staring off into what Maxine called "a hole in the world." It was exactly where Rose felt she now lived, in a hole in the world.

Alice made Rose wash her face, hands, and teeth. Alice helped her into her boots, tied her laces, buttoned her dress. Told her she was being an excellent walnut. And to keep going. Alice said they just needed to keep going. The school was a good place for keeping going. The whistles blew, the hands clapped, and Rose pissed and dressed and walked and ate and worked and slept. She kept going.

It was raining as they headed out to the circles. Not much. More like the sky was spitting, and not like it was crying as hard as Rose had that first day during periodic excusing, when Alice had shaken her. Reminding her, stern and mean-like, about the keeping going and how walnuts didn't cry.

As Rose walked the circle, the sky spitting down on her, she felt the heaviness of the rocks lift just a little. Rose walked and walked as the sun struggled to rise behind a giant wall of gray clouds. She walked curve after curve, bend after bend, and remembered her friend.

London.

Gone forever.

It had been two nights now, and she hadn't been caught. She'd done it. Even without Rose's nickels or the stolen dress. She'd made it.

Alice said that two nights didn't mean she wouldn't be caught, but two nights did mean she wasn't likely to be caught. That meant London had likely made it. Christmas Day. It had been a good plan. A plan Rose had helped with. No one went looking. They were busy singing and eating. Busy celebrating the birth of a baby . . . like the one London had told Rose she was going to have.

Rose walked the circles in the rain and thought about London. She thought about the baby. Coming in the springtime. She didn't think about Maxine or the cages. Not while she walked the circles. She thought about Maxine every other place, but the circles she gave to London. Because London had loved them.

"Rose," she'd said one afternoon while they'd walked. "How can you not like this?"

London loved how the paths started at no place and ended at no place. They just went on and on. "Round," London had said, "like the sun and the moon and the earth."

"What about the stars?" Rose had asked her. "Stars aren't round. And they're much prettier than the sun. You can't even look at the sun."

"The shine around a star is a little bit round," London had argued.

They'd decided they had both been right. Stars were prettier than the sun, and though they weren't round like the paths, they did shine in a circle.

Later that day, back at afternoon circles, Rose smiled up at the rain still falling from the sky. Soon there'd be stars. Soon Maxine would come home. Soon

London would have a tiny baby. So many happy things to look forward to on a gray and lonely day. Alice was right. Keep going. Keep walking. And walking and walking and walking.

The rain fell. And Rose shivered. It was cold. Her head felt cold on the inside, behind her forehead. She stumbled on the path.

Alice steadied her from behind.

"Do you see the stars, London?"

"Rose?"

Rose laughed. Alice wasn't London. She didn't know why she'd said that. It was her head, feeling like it ached. Her throat, too. It hurt when she swallowed her mouth water. It had hurt when she'd woken up this morning.

Because Maxxie wasn't there again.

And London was far away. With the old lady who sat by the window and called everyone bad names. The lady London loved.

Now Rose did see stars. She was sure of it.

"Maxine?"

"No, baby, it's me," Alice said.

She was taking Rose's stick. Why was Alice taking her stick?

"Rose," Alice whispered. "You're sick. Miss Sweeney went for the matron. I'll keep your stick safe."

"With the book?"

"With the book. When you're well, Maxine and I will be here. Waiting for you."

Alice squeezed Rose's fingers then, something Rose had seen Maxine do to Alice. Squeeze her fingers. Rose didn't cry.

Walnuts didn't cry.

London took the punches and the kicks. The cops beat it out of her, the pain. Right there on Decatur Street. In the gutter. Not far from where she'd thrown up. It felt like ages ago that she'd put Alby down with that kick on this same stretch of sidewalk.

She knew he'd done it. Alby had told his father she was pregnant, and the cops had come for her. The hardworking and respectable Flannery family had removed the threat of the knocked-up dago bitch. They needn't have worried. She would have never married Alby, that egg.

The cops grew tired, sweaty, hungry. They tossed her into the back and locked her in. She heard them laughing, drinking. Smelled the cigarettes and the whiskey and the black peppery aroma of culatello as she bounced about in the back on the floor. She'd been here before. Twice before. And now they were taking her back.

It had been her plan. Where else could she go?

No clams and a sandbar.

She would have Rose, and her baby. She'd ask Maxine to forgive her. She'd never done that before, said she was sorry. She'd never felt sorry—at least she didn't think she had—though she'd done a hundred shitty things in her life.

The truck hit a nasty pothole, and London's head smacked the metal floor. She remembered the girl in the iron lung. Three months now. Three months the girl had been inside her metal lung. Three months since London realized she was pregnant. The girl lay locked away in some room somewhere, and soon London would be locked away as well. But she wouldn't stay there forever. She vowed it, as the wagon rumbled and sputtered her closer and closer. She'd have the baby and figure it out. Figure it out for the both of them. Without the old lady.

Screw that old lady.

But London didn't feel it. The anger. She just felt the pain . . . and told herself it came from her broken nose, her bruised ribs, her aching head.

They yanked her out and walked her in. There was the signing off on the paper, and the attendants—two different women this time—and the walk down the stairs, keys jangling. The smells hit London just as hard as they had the last time. There wasn't any getting used to a stench that bad. Same doors to unlock, open, close, and lock. Same dim hallways. Same rooms to pass. Same moans. Although, this time the attendants carried her under each of her arms, gingerly, kindly. London figured she must really look like hell.

Finally they led her into a cell. Laid her on the piss-soaked mattress. It was like an awful-smelling homecoming. They hovered in the doorway, watching her. She closed her eyes, hurting too much to care.

A third woman entered. It was the attendant with the gray hair. The one who lived here like London lived here. She knelt on the floor, dipped a cloth into a washbasin, and brought it to London's bloody face. London flinched, not from pain but from pleasure. The water was warm. The cloth was soft. The gray-haired woman washed London's face. She cut off the overalls and the nightclothes, bloodied, from her nose maybe, or her teeth. London was sure one of those buzzers had knocked out a tooth or two.

Then she dressed her. Fed her warm soup. Brushed her hair. Braided it. Covered her with a blanket. And left her to sleep.

London slept, waking once in the night when she made the mistake of turning her face toward the mattress, the putrid smell yanking her awake. Pointing her nose back up at the ceiling, and breathing in through all the hurt, she tumbled back into the black of sleep.

Just as they had done the last time she'd been caged, they allowed her to sleep through the first day. Feeding her. But no more washbasins filled with warm water showed up. The second morning, when she heard breakfast on the way, she hoped to hell they'd pass her by. Let her be.

But the guards came for her.

London struggled to her feet. Her stomach cramping in pain. Her head begging to stay stuck to the pissy mattress. Those pricks. They'd done her over badly. There wasn't any place that wasn't sore and bruised.

The women walked in a line just as they had before. They sat on the bench. London kept her head down because she actually couldn't pick it up. Or focus her eyes. The shit buckets of the Back Ward weren't something anyone wanted to focus on anyway.

London accepted her bucket, slipped to her knees, and began to shuffle about picking up shit, wiping up piss, passing the feet of women strewn about on the benches or wafting past her like ghosts. She was thankful to be on her knees instead of struggling to stand upright with a hose in hand inside the showers. It was a thoughtless job, and London didn't think. Couldn't think. Not past trying to keep moving.

How long she'd been working or hovering above the filthy floorboards when she felt the bleeding, she didn't know. It began as a terrible pulling from deep inside her. Like her stomach had turned to poison and her body was attempting to shove it out of her. She leaned on her bucket and breathed through the pain as it moved from her stomach up into her chest and head like a screaming February wind. Then came the warm wetness between her legs. Scratchy. How could blood be scratchy?

Maxine was beside her then. Pulling her to her feet.

Standing released the blood, and it ran down her legs. There was an attendant, and Maxine. And now a toilet room, with a row of sinks and toilets just like in their dormitory. London, in all her pain, couldn't help wondering why the women of the Back Ward couldn't just shit in here.

They hiked up her dress. Placed her on a toilet, where London slumped over her knees. She heard the door lock and wondered if she was alone.

"It's okay."

Maxine.

London could hear herself moaning. The cramping was god-awful, like her menses had come and was seriously huffed. The pain bubbled, hotter and hotter, and London reached for Maxine in an effort to stop it.

Maxine understood, and she held on to London as wave after horrible wave ripped through her body . . . until finally—she noticed it first in the coolness of her forehead, and then immediately in the bottom of her stomach—London felt it ending. Felt it leave her. Not as one thing but as many, hot, wet, painful things. Maxine held on to her, and London held back. Held her so tightly, in fact, that Maxine's shoulders had trouble heaving as she cried. London wanted to cry too. She wanted to cry more than anything else she'd ever wanted in her entire life, which seriously had never been much. Instead she clung to Maxine until the girl's weeping shuddered to a stop.

Maxine leaned back, her watery eyes looking deeply into London's. London held her gaze. The girl kneeling before her was thin and pale, her eyes sunk deeply into her face. How long had she been in the cages? How long had it been since that other terrible moment—when Rose had sobbed and Maxine, screeching, had been bound up and dragged away?

"It was my fault," London whispered. "Not Alice's. Mine."

Maxine shook her head. "Not now."

"But, Maxine—"

Maxine cut her off by sliding from her knees into a sitting position on the tiled floor, letting her head hang slack on her neck, and her hair fall across her face. She looked even thinner in this small human heap. But worse than this, she looked empty.

"Maxine," London repeated, a feeling of desperation crawling up her throat.

The girl didn't move.

London knew this world was crap. Just as the old woman always said. But, God, did it always have to be? Couldn't some little piece of it not be?

"I know you love her. Please, Maxine." London hardly recognized her own voice bleating like a goat in her ears. "Don't stop loving her."

Now Maxine straightened, her eyes lit with anger.

"Why did everyone know about the money and the dress but me? Why?"

Anger was good. Anger wasn't empty.

"Just knowing things means shit, Maxine. Absolute shit. But knowing the right thing to do, here, in a place like this . . . that's something none of us knows." The truth of her own words stunned her. Had she ever in her whole goddamn life known the right thing to do?

But she could still see the pain in Maxine's eyes.

"Alice didn't know what to do, Maxine. She just didn't know what to do."

"I know," Maxine conceded, covering her face with both her hands and taking in a big breath. "I know." She dropped her hands then and looked directly at London. "But now *we* need to do something." She climbed back to her knees and began gathering toilet paper. "There isn't much time."

She handed the paper to London, and London placed it between her legs with pressure, letting the blood soak into the paper. Maxine went for more, wet some at the sinks to clean the blood from London's legs, removed London's blood-soaked underwear. When it was time for London to stand, she found she couldn't, and Maxine took her arm and lifted her from the toilet.

"Don't turn around," Maxine told her. And London didn't.

"Okay. Now," she whispered.

London turned.

Maxine held a tiny red bundle wrapped in London's underwear. A baby. Her baby. She had spent so much time trying not to think about it, and now, being separated from it, she regretted how she'd wasted that time. Regretted it terribly.

Maxine's eyes searched the room. "Listen, we've got to hide it. We'll come back for it later."

"We'll never be back here," London said. "You know that."

Maxine frowned, ignoring her.

A key clicked in the lock, and Maxine and London turned toward it.

The door opened. An attendant stood in the doorframe holding a towel, with a menstrual rag and clean underwear sitting on top of it. She stared at the two girls standing shoulder to shoulder in the toilet room, and took in what Maxine held in her hands.

Stepping inside, she placed the rag and the underwear on the sink, and then ripped the towel in two. "Give it to me," she said.

Neither girl moved.

"It will be buried. As proper as I can do it on my own."

Again the girls didn't move.

"Listen," the attendant said, looking behind her to be sure they were alone. "There's two other ways this can go. Both of them bad. I'll do as I said. I'll lay the little thing to rest, best I can."

Maxine turned to London.

London nodded, and so Maxine placed the bundle on the towel.

"Where?" London asked.

"On the grounds," the attendant said, immediately understanding what London needed to hear. "But I won't tell you exactly where. I can't have you trying to visit it. They'd let me go for sure, and I need this job." She gently folded the baby into the towel.

It was then that London felt as if she'd just put down something very heavy. Her eyesight darkened, and her legs shook.

The attendant closely considered London for the first time since she'd entered the room. "You okay?" she asked.

"I'm fine," London answered.

It was a lie. And it made London feel so good to tell it. More like herself. Until her knees buckled.

Alice was alone for five nights. The longest nights she'd ever spent since her very first night in the dormitory, when every cough or sigh had sent her heart racing. If she had been anyone else on that first long, lonely night, she might have wished herself home, or off in some magical place. But Alice wasn't anyone else, and she lay, heart racing, wishing for nothing.

On this fifth night alone as she stared up into the blackness hovering over her cot, she realized that she *had* been wishing for something that first night. It was the same something she wished for now: to disappear.

Wishing Maxine back, on the cot next to her, was something she didn't do. Especially now, with Rose in the Sick Ward. She couldn't live without Maxine, and Maxine couldn't live without Rose. So Alice found herself once again lying in the dark and asking it to swallow her.

The dark did not comply, and exactly ten minutes

before the whistle blew, Alice opened her eyes, as she always did.

Sitting in periodic excusing, she again counted the things she'd done wrong. Letting Rose collect her stolen items. Not telling Maxine. Forcing Rose into her shell. Why did she see it all so clearly now when she couldn't before? Because she was just what they always said she was, a moron. A moron who was slowly becoming an imbecile . . . who would soon be an idiot.

Four claps.

Keep going.

Alice kept going. Like the sun moved across the sky, she moved through each day, walking, blinking, breathing, but not living. Keeping going didn't include living.

During morning circles, Mary came up on her. Walked next to her. They almost never interacted, she and Mary. Both of them understood that one black girl was hard enough for this world to deal with. Two together was too much. But Mary did it. Without a word. Reminding Alice that she wasn't alone. Reminding Alice to keep walking.

During sewing, Helen plucked the trousers from Alice's lap to finish the hem when they'd lain there too long. Another time, a frayed collar. Keep sewing.

Frances placed her apple on Alice's lunch tray. Keep eating.

Dottie hummed next to her as they worked the mangle during Manual Training. Keep working.

And Edwina sat her quiet self closely next to Alice on the benches that evening. Keep breathing.

All of it. All of them. Kept Alice going.

Sitting by her window, Alice simmered in worry. Seven days and nights in the cages. When would this end? What would Maxine be like after so much time in the Back Ward? Would there be an eighth night? And Rose. Fevers could worsen. Could Maxine be in the Sick Ward now too? The idea of Alice's old worry, the one where they all grew up and were separated, seemed like something out of the wonderful dream in which Maxine sang. Alice would take that worry in a heartbeat. But unlike the circular paths, life kept moving in a forward motion. There was no going back.

"Maxine!" Neddie cried.

Ragno clapped her hands three times mightily at the outburst, but Alice's heart had already started beating wildly.

She hadn't been looking. Didn't look up now. Couldn't.

She felt Edwina move away. Felt the cold absence. Felt Maxine sit. Felt Maxine's thigh press lightly, so very lightly, against her own, and she knew. It was over, Maxine's anger. It was over. Maxine had returned. And she didn't hate Alice. Never had hated her. But the relief was short. Because of Rose.

Alice could feel Maxine searching for her.

The room was quiet. So quiet that Alice could hear herself blink. Everyone was watching, though all eyes faced the wall across from the benches on which the girls sat, as per the rules. But eyes didn't have to be trained on a thing to see. Eyes were able to take in from their sides, from their tops, from their bottoms. So many eyes . . . all of them curious but not all of them kind. Alice didn't move.

But she felt.

Alice felt the day her brother dropped her off. She felt that first dark night on the cot. She felt, always. The soft nut inside her pulsed against her hard shell. It threatened to break open those seams. Expose her. She blinked. And blinked. Her mouth filled with water. She blinked again.

She had to tell Maxine. A small trickle of sweat ran down her back. Alice straightened against the bench. The movement was too much, and she cleared her throat.

The eyes snapped over, not being able to control themselves against this new sound. Alice felt a small crack in the back of her head. And then another two cracks. Ragno. Clapping. Four claps this time. Saving her.

Everyone stood. Everyone lined up. Everyone walked to the toilets. Alice was part of everyone. Walking. Keeping going. She leaned in before she could stop herself.

"In the Sick Ward. With a fever."

Maxine's shoulders stiffened. But she kept walking. Kept going. Alice followed. Into the toilets, where the lock turned in the door and the girls were alone.

Maxine turned to Alice. "What happened?"

"Walking the circles. It was cold, and raining. Five days ago. They took her."

Maxine moaned, and dropped onto a toilet, her head in her hands. "Five days. Alone. She won't get well. She will look for me and look for me. And I'm not there. I can't be there." She hopped from the toilet, the idea of Rose alone in the Sick Ward too much to bear in a sitting position.

"Rose can't be alone." Maxine's voice was high-pitched, and Alice saw that it wasn't only Rose who feared being without her sister. Alice longed to comfort Maxine, to tell her she wasn't alone, that Alice would always be here for her. She would have said so many things, but words were never something she had many of. And touching—Alice could feel Ellen watching.

But then Maxine's face twisted into a strange look of joy. "London," she choked. "London is there. In the Sick Ward. With Rose."

"London?"

"She didn't make it. They got her. She, she"—here Maxine stopped, became careful—"was beat up badly. She collapsed. She's with Rose."

Alice couldn't believe they'd caught London. She'd felt sure London had made it. The strangest thought occurred to her then, that London had returned because Rose was sick. But Alice knew this was complete applesauce. London could not have known. Alice just didn't want to be what this place said she was . . . what this place said they all were. She wanted London to prove them wrong. Because she knew she herself never would.

"She'll be okay. Rose will be okay. Right, Alice? Right?"

Maxine said this while she searched Alice's face, and Alice knew that her next words needed to be chosen very carefully, lest she lie to Maxine. She couldn't lie to Maxine. Not now. Not about Rose.

"London won't let anyone hurt her."

Maxine smiled. Alice had never seen anything more beautiful.

That night, Alice was not alone. She lay watching Maxine on the cot next to her, sleeping the sleep of the exhausted, from a week in the cages, a week of hard labor and of harder circumstances. Maxine was wrapped up in her blanket, with Rose's stick clutched to her breast. And when Alice opened her eyes ten minutes before the whistle, she made her first hopeful wish.

That this would be the day Rose and London came home.

London drifted in and out of sleep. When she drifted out, and the lights and sounds of the real world began to make themselves known, she'd quickly drift back in.

In was nice. In was free. From an old woman. From a milquetoast boy. From a tiny bloody bundle.

Eventually the real world held on to her longer and longer—with its obnoxious bright lights, and its cold piss, and its shouts and sobs and suffering. London understood where she was. The Sick Ward. She also understood the danger she was in. Her father had gone to the hospital and never returned.

Lying still and quiet and needing nothing, a kind of torpor came over her. She imagined that the world felt it too, and would leave her on this corner cot to waste away at her own pace. Most all of her was fine with this, just not her goddamn stomach. When an attendant came rolling a cart of oatmeal near her,

London reached for it, and thus began her reluctant recovery.

On the first day she could fully remember, she ate breakfast, took note of the large room full of bodies in beds, and knowingly pissed her sheets, whereas previously she'd done it unawares. By the second day, the sheer misery of lying in her own blood and piss forced her onto the chamber pot, which in turn led to eating all three meals as they were offered. She was still bleeding, and her stomach cramping, although not as badly as it had in the toilets of the Back Ward. Those toilets. Her mind would often flit there—to the gray tile, and the attendant with her towel—but it refused to ever land.

By the third day, she was sick to death of lying in her own mess. Throwing off her putrid blanket, she went in search of fresh nightclothes and a menstrual rag . . . and found Rose.

"Rose!"

The girl didn't stir, and London touched her face, then jerked back her hand. Rose was hotter than a coal fire.

"Rose?" London whispered.

London looked around for a nurse, knowing it was useless, then turned to the sick lying nearby, as if any of them might know something, anything, about her friend. Hopeless, London turned back to the only one who could help her understand what was happening.

"Rose," she begged. "Rose, can you hear me? It's

London. I'm here. Right here." She picked up Rose's hot hand and held it.

An attendant swung by. "I wouldn't touch her if I were you. She's burning with fever."

"Do I look like you?" London snapped.

Too busy, the woman didn't even stop to reprimand her.

"London?"

"Rose," London gasped, turning back to the cot. "Rose, yes. It's me. I'm here."

Rose smiled but seemed too weak to open her eyes. "I knew you'd come visit me."

"Visit?"

"We made a good plan, right? Christmas."

Shit. Rose didn't understand that London was back inside.

"London?"

"I'm here."

"Do you have water to share?"

"I'll get you water. I'll be right back."

She let go of Rose's hand and wandered toward a set of open double doors, passing cot after cot, each containing a small mound of humanity twisted up in dirty blankets and smelling like browning broccoli.

Rose was sick because of what had happened. Sick over Maxine thrown to the ground, trussed like a pig in that straitjacket. Sick because she'd tried to help *London.*

Passing through the double doors, London entered

an entirely new room, this one filled with more cots, more sick people. She hurried through this second room toward two large sideboards piled with clean laundry, but no water, and no one to ask about it.

She needed to think but couldn't. Not in all this filth. Without further deliberation she stripped off her foul nightclothes and pulled on fresh ones and then ripped a sheet in two, and tied it around her like underwear to stop the flow of blood between her thighs. She felt so much better. Taking in her surroundings, she braided her hair, and bound it with another ripped piece of sheet.

She left the middle sick room through another set of wide-open double doors beside the sideboards, and found herself in a hall across from a third set of double doors, but these doors were closed. To her right the hallway ended in a wall, and to her left it led to two different doors—one of them most likely the exit and most likely locked. London tried the double doors. They were unlocked.

This room was filled with cribs . . . twenty, maybe thirty of them, and yet was eerily quiet. Curtains were drawn across the large windows, creating a thick gloom that mixed with the heavy silence, making it seem like the air in the room wouldn't support sound even if it were to happen. But there was a sink. In the far, right corner.

Strangely, London couldn't move. Those cribs weren't empty. She could smell them. Babies. A mix of ammonia, wet cloth, and old shit. What kind of babies lay in a dark room without crying? Thirty of them, no less.

"Watch out."

London stumbled out of the way of an attendant whisking past her into the room carrying a stack of clean towels.

"I'm thirsty," London called out.

"Well, you can see the sink," the woman answered.

"A cup?"

"What are you, a Rockefeller? Stick your head under the faucet."

"It's for someone else."

The woman stopped and turned, taking in London standing in her nightclothes. "You sick?"

"Lost a baby," she said, liking the sound of the word "lost." As if one day, when she was ready, she might find it.

"Still bleeding?"

"Yes."

"Bright or dark?"

"Dark."

The woman stared at her, thinking. "Okay, follow me."

London stepped into the room, letting the doors close quietly behind her. Everything in here seemed to happen in a dense hush. After tiptoeing to the nearest crib, she stared down at the child. Naked except for a diaper, and sound asleep, the baby was large-headed, like Lizzie, only not like Lizzie in that its head ballooned twelve inches over its brows.

London looked into the next crib. Two bright eyes looked back. Eyes not separated by a nose but by a small flap of skin, no lips, ears located too close to its chin, and tiny fists clenched into what looked to London like small, pink knots. The baby gurgled, waving its arms about, and London longed to reach out, and when she realized she could, there was nothing so softly beautiful as the child's fingers grasping her own.

"Hello, you sloppy little noodle," she cooed. "What's your name?"

The attendant sighed, shifting the towels she'd been holding to her hip, and walked to the end of the baby's crib. Squinting down at a chart stuck to its footboard, she read. *"Miriam."*

"Miriam," London repeated, picking the baby out of the crib like she'd done it a thousand times.

"Careful," the woman said. "She's terminal."

"Terminal?"

The attendant sighed again. "Born with ailments that can't be cured. She's dying, is the crop of it. All of 'em are."

"You don't look dying to me," London told Miriam. Miriam spit up.

"Although, you are disgusting," London laughed, holding Miriam and her spit at arm's length.

The woman tossed London a clean towel and watched as she gently wiped Miriam's mouth and chin. Shaking her head, the attendant walked to the sink and filled a metal pitcher with water, and then dug a cup from a cabinet.

London held the baby up to her face. "See you, Miriam," she whispered, then placed her back in the crib and gave Miriam's warm belly a final pat before thanking the woman for the water.

She spent the rest of the afternoon sitting next to a feverish Rose, who did not wake again. When the claps came for the shift change and dinner, London squeezed Rose's hand, which reminded her of Miriam's tiny fist, and returned to her cot.

She lay in her sodden sheets until dinner came around, and grabbed the bread from the plate before it was even out of the attendant's hand.

"You look well enough to me," the woman spat, moving on.

Crap, thought London as she poured her soup down her throat. She should have pretended to be asleep or been groaning in pain. Tomorrow they'd be handing her a shit bucket for sure.

Later that night when the lights went out, she climbed from her cot and went to Rose. London's eyes had adjusted to the dark room, and the light from the almost full moon shone across the sick. Rose was still sleeping, and still hot to the touch. London soaked a rag in the metal pitcher of water she'd hidden under Rose's cot and placed it on the girl's forehead.

"Rose," she sighed, not expecting Rose to answer, and she didn't. All around her, the sick lay strewn about on their cots, shifting, moaning, trying to find comfort in an uncomfortable place. London was thankful that Rose slept. She needed rest. And Maxine. How could London make sure she got both?

She stood by Rose until her thoughts turned to a baby tucked in a towel and an old woman missing from a window, and then London drifted back to her cot and slept.

Sneaking out before breakfast, she went and found the woman in with the babies.

"What do you want?"

London wanted this woman to get her assigned to Manual Training in Sick Ward. But she had no idea how to get this done or if this woman even had the authority to do it . . . or whether she would do it if she could.

"Not a goddamn thing," London said, wandering over to Miriam's crib.

There she was again, that little kipper, looking up at her. London smiled.

"You got someone in Sick Ward?" the woman asked.

"Yeah," London said.

The woman went back to work, keeping her eye on London as the girl played with the baby.

"She shit her diaper," London called.

The woman made her way over to London with a

bucket, rags, and a fresh diaper. Her name was Gladys. She showed London how to remove Miriam's rubber pants, unpin the diaper, wash her bum, and pin on a fresh diaper.

"If you're feeling up to it, I could use the help," Gladys said.

"I guess I could change a few of these little turds." Yet even as the words left her mouth, she was already reaching for the next baby as if she were dying to wipe their yippy little asses . . . and maybe she was.

By lunch London mostly had the hang of it. She'd only poked one or two tiny thighs with a safety pin and had figured out how to get tight rubber pants on and off squirming baby bodies with their floppy legs.

"Wash up and go eat," Gladys told her.

"Not hungry," London said, sure she'd find a couple of goons waiting at her cot, ready to take her back to the cages.

"You know," Gladys said, "Sick Ward's not anyone's choice."

London looked over at her but didn't say anything.

"I could request you for Manual Training."

"I'm fucking starving," London said. "I'll be back after lunch."

London couldn't believe it. She might be able to stay with Rose . . . and Miriam. She ate her lunch, and then stopped by to see Rose, who didn't look like she'd stirred all morning. London managed to get a little water down Rose's throat, changed Rose's sheets and nightclothes, and brushed her hair with her fingers as best she could, which wasn't that well. Rose mostly slept through the care. Since London was still hungry, she ate Rose's lunch. One of the nurses caught her with a mouthful of stew.

"Put that down."

London put it down. But as soon as the nurse turned her back, London picked it right back up and finished it in two bites. "I'll be back soon," she whispered into Rose's ear.

The crib room was almost always empty but for the babies, and Gladys coming and going. London could see now why they never cried or fussed. There was no one to hear them in this lonely, dark room.

Gladys taught her how to feed them a liquid poured from tins into bottles. It looked like milk but wasn't. London tasted it. It was nasty. But these little bananas seemed to like it, even if eating was difficult for many of them. Their mouths didn't work quite right, or their stomachs, or their noses, and there was a lot of spit and vomit and snot and frustration. But Gladys had lent London an apron, and so she held the babies tightly against her and patiently worked the bottles in and out of their mouths, adjusting and wiping.

When the four claps rang out, London was shocked at how fast the day had gone. Gladys stood across the room, a diaper over one shoulder, baby feet in her hands.

"Git."

"Will I be back?"

"I wrote up the paperwork for Mrs. Vetter. It's all I can do."

London reached down into Miriam's crib and gently squeezed her big toe. Then she hung her apron and walked out of the crib room.

Wearing the wool dress of the degenerate and standing on line with the other girls brought in for Manual Training, she was marched out of the large North Building that housed the Sick Ward and down the path toward the dormitory. Just as London had suspected, she had been deemed healthy and was being returned to regular life within the institution. She tried to ignore the ache in her chest as she moved farther from Rose and the babies. She'd be back. Gladys had written up the paperwork, and this place loved its paperwork.

But before she entered the dining hall, Ragno caught sight of her, and the nasty bitch insisted on having the matron called, along with Mrs. Vetter.

London once again found herself in the tiny office-like room in the front of the dormitory, where she'd first arrived and taken the test about fast-moving trains and little girls cut up into pieces. She sat alone, the desk nurse having gone off to fetch Vetter and the matron, leaving her purse hanging on the back of the chair. *Ridiculous*, London thought, and she briskly relieved the woman of half the money in it. A sawbuck and change, no less. The nurse would think she'd lost it or overspent somewhere. Because what moron wouldn't take all the money?

It was another five minutes before the nurse returned. In that time, it took every ounce of restraint London had not to steal more money, along with the nurse's lipstick, just because she could.

Mrs. Vetter assumed command of the chair across from London. She had a file folder in her hand—most likely all the notes they'd taken on London since she'd arrived. London couldn't help wondering if her baby was in there. She liked the idea of it being written down. Permanently, in ink. The matron and desk nurse did not sit, but stood next to Mrs. Vetter, knowing their place.

"Dear," began Mrs. Vetter. London could see that the head nurse was angry, and she quickly decided that no matter what this woman said, she would say nothing. Absolutely nothing. If she wanted to help Rose, or see Miriam again, London had to keep her mouth shut.

"First you get yourself in trouble, and now I hear you've lost the child. Well, no one can say that it isn't for the best. God knows, we don't need another generation of mental defectives."

London dropped her face to the floor so that the woman wouldn't catch the hatred burning in her eyes.

"You're here, dear, so that we may help protect you from your own moral weaknesses. Do you understand?"

London needed to respond. She needed this woman to approve Gladys's request that London be allowed to work in the Sick Ward. But there was no way she could look up at this woman without telling her to go to hell. Instead she dropped her head even lower, as a sign she understood.

It worked.

"That's better. Now, be thankful you're here in Massachusetts. Almost any other state would have you sterilized, as well you should be. Motherhood is a privilege, my dear, not a right."

The woman took a deep, cleansing breath to transition from her lecture to London's file. "I had hoped," she said, filtering through the papers, "that you'd become a finished worker here at the Fernald School. You tested as a high-grade moron upon entry, but I can see now that this is obviously inaccurate, and that Nurse Gamble here"—she nodded toward the standing nurse—"will need to retest you in the next few weeks, and I'm sure it will be proved that in truth you are an imbecile."

London knew she would be failing this next test, confirming this woman's assumptions; anything else would bring her trouble.

"Well, we shall make do with what we have, my dear. And in the least, make a rough worker out of you." She closed the file on her lap, folded her hands on top of it, and now sat looking at London.

The girl stopped breathing. She had vowed to stay

quiet. To get back to Rose. And this woman held that decision in her neatly folded hands.

"The truth of the matter is," continued the head nurse, "we've found that imbeciles minister well to their idiot brothers and sisters. I see that Gladys has requested your services, and under her direction I'm sure you'll find that the Sick Ward's monotonous round of simple daily avocations will not only keep you from lapsing into idiocy but may end up giving you a sort of happiness and true sense of home."

London kept her head down. Silence. It could mean anything, but London knew exactly how Mrs. Vetter was taking hers . . . as an acquiescence. Not that London gave a pig's pizzle, just as long as she was able to see Rose the next day.

"Wait here for a moment while I speak with the matron and Nurse Gamble. The nurse will schedule your next round of testing, and then you can head up to dinner."

Mrs. Vetter rose from her chair and exited the office, followed by the matron and the nurse.

They stood a few feet from the door.

"I'm disappointed in your results, Mrs. Gamble," Mrs. Vetter said. "You must have administered the test incorrectly." She went on to chastise the nurse within London's earshot. Nurse Gamble, realizing this, pulled the office door shut.

Left alone with the purse once again, London rolled her eyes, and then quickly stole the lipstick.

Maxine saw London before Alice did. Across the dining room. The need to run to her was overwhelming, and she bobbed in her seat, but it was against the rules to move from the table.

Being London, she went for her dinner first, and then headed for Maxine. It was the longest wait of Maxine's life. She attempted to determine Rose's condition by London's walk toward her . . . to know her sister was okay from the swing of the girl's hair, how low her shoulders rested, the speed of her gait.

"I've seen her. She's got a fever. I don't know how bad it is," London said, before she even placed her tray down.

A rush of tears came to Maxine's eyes. Was it relief? Yes. Had she thought that her little sister was dead? She didn't know. Probably. So many inmates died in Sick Ward. So many.

Her head still aching from fear, she watched

London eat her dinner, biting into her bread from the side of her mouth like a dog and chewing with a wide-open mouth. The claps were coming. Dinner was almost over. As hard as it was, Maxine waited for more information.

The claps came. Maxine's heart fell.

London dumped the last of her soup into her mouth, not bothering with the spoon, wiped her lips with her dress sleeve, burped, and then said, "I'm going back tomorrow. And every day after that. They've given me Sick Ward as Manual Training."

Now Maxine cried. Into her napkin. And then into London's, since London hadn't used it. She cried all the way to the day room. Alice walked slowly in front of her in line to shield her from Bessie's and Ellen's view. Crying was a sign of weakness, a sign to attack. But they'd be wrong to think Maxine felt weak. She didn't. She felt strong. Rose was alive. And London would make sure she stayed that way. She'd bring Rose home.

No. Not home. Back to the dormitory. Maxine would bring Rose home, just as she'd always promised she would.

Never one to hold back, Maxine leaned into Alice and London as they entered the day room, whispering hoarsely, "We're leaving. As soon as Rose is well."

She was breathless from these few words, and she teetered some as she made her way through the door. Saying it made it real. No matter that London rolled her eyes. Alice didn't. In fact, Alice flinched. A beautiful flinch. A joyful flinch. A flinch that had Maxine dreaming before her bum hit the bench. Not about her home in Somerville. Not about her mother coming for them. Not about sitting on those damn couches in the visiting room, but about eloping. All four of them. Together.

She skipped the part about how they'd do it and went straight to the part where they were all living together in a large house. By the sea. Listening to the waves at night in their beds and breathing in the salty air. Maybe they'd even take a swim, come summer when the water was warm. Yes, they were leaving this place. Soon.

"She needs her stick," London said.

Rose had now been in the Sick Ward with rheumatic fever for a month. London had heard the diagnosis from the nurses. Rose was red and blotchy and still feverish, but talking, and even eating a little. Maxine loved hearing about the eating. Rose must have been feeling better if she was eating.

"How come they won't let me work there too, so I can see her?" Maxine asked, though she absolutely knew why she wasn't allowed to work in the Sick Ward.

"Gotta be an imbecile," London said, soup dribbling down her chin, "like me."

The three of them were huddled close at the end of a dining table. Meals were one of the few times when talking was openly allowed.

"It's wrong not to let me visit," Maxine complained. But no one was allowed to visit the Sick Ward, for fear of epidemics. Besides fire, it was the institution's biggest fear.

"Let me have her stick," persisted London. She had been asking for Rose's stick for weeks, but Maxine hesitated to let go of the only piece she had left of her sister. "It will help her. I know it."

Maxine relented. "Take it on Monday."

Alice pursed her lips.

"It's okay, Alice," Maxine said. "London won't let anyone find it." And without thinking, she reached out to touch Alice's hand.

Alice snatched up her spoon, and London squinted a warning at Maxine.

Bruised, even if she did understand, Maxine moved past it by launching into her new favorite topic of conversation. "Let's talk about the plan."

"You've got to dry that shit up," London snapped. "Those two ass scratchers are always listening."

The three girls couldn't help themselves, and they glanced down the table at Bessie and Ellen.

Ellen sneered back, and London itched to give her the finger, but didn't. "Screw those bims," she said. "Anyway, the kind of fever Rose has takes a real long time to heal. The nurses say it hurts the heart, and even when the fever breaks, Rose's heart will need time. A lot of time. You gonna eat the rest of your bread?"

"I know," Maxine grumbled, ignoring the bread request. "You've already told me." London was always meaner on Fridays. The girl hated the weekend. Maxine leaned in closer and whispered, "We shouldn't think about going to the *beach* until summer anyway; just like you said, it's always nicer in warm weather. We've got plenty of time. We don't turn fifteen until the fall—"

"Tomorrow is choir," Alice interrupted, changing the subject.

Maxine smiled, and let herself be distracted. She had been allowed to continue with her piano lessons before choir practice. According to Miss Petruskavich, Maxine was becoming quite good. She was going to play the organ for the Hallelujah Chorus from Handel's *Messiah* at Easter, which was the last day of March, nine weeks away. Her only hope was that her sister would be well enough to come and hear her play.

God, she missed Rose. The pain of it felt like she'd swallowed a hunk of apple and it had lodged itself behind her collarbone. No amount of time spent at the piano was worth it if Rose wasn't there.

The claps sounded for Manual Training.

"I know what you just did, Alice," Maxine said, collecting her tray and standing. "I don't know why you two don't like the beach."

"We do like the beach," London said. "Everybody likes the lousy beach."

It was true. London and Alice had been helping with the plan. It had been Alice's idea to stash the money they'd stolen in an old borax detergent box. Alice had then hidden it outside the back door of the washing room, where the attendants and maintenance men hung out, smoking and flirting. She was made to clean up the old butts a few times a day and had found it easy to bury the box under the rocks near the maple tree.

Eleven dollars and seventy-eight cents. It was more money than Maxine had ever seen in her entire life. And they'd stolen it. Together.

Well, not exactly together, but as a team. A team led heavily by London, who had stolen eleven dollars and sixty-seven cents of it. Alice had found a penny in the pocket of one of the outside dresses she'd been hand-washing, and Maxine had discovered two nickels that Ragno had missed when she'd cleaned out the vent.

The claps sounded a second time. Ellen and Bessie got up and made sure to pass closely by the three girls, Bessie shoving Maxine into the table as she passed.

"Come push *me*, bitch," London spat.

In an attempt to refocus London, Maxine kept planning as they joined the line. It was Miss Sweeney today, so they took their time. "We need to step up our search for clams," she said.

London, cramming the rest of Maxine's bread into her mouth, eyeballed her.

"Okay," Maxine said, "*I* need to step up my search for clams."

They all knew Alice couldn't. Getting caught doing anything wrong would be far worse for Alice than it would be for them. It would mean another long trip to the cages. Or worse. They'd often heard the rumors of girls being sent to the state prison a half day's drive to the west, even if they'd never known anyone to go.

"We'll only need enough to get by for a month," Maxine said. "After that we'll have jobs and the rent won't be a problem. How much is rent again, London?"

"A sawbuck or two. For a dump. But I already told you, if we look suspicious, which we will, they're going to shake us down for more."

"Twenty dollars," Maxine moaned. "How will we *ever* find that much?"

"More like thirty," London said. "We'll need to eat."

The girls shut up then and found their places in line. They would now walk together out of the dining hall and outside the building, where they'd break apart for Manual Training. Maxine was still in the clothing room because of Rose. At the Fernald School, routine and regiment were as important as breathing, and once a thing had been written down, it entered a realm akin to holiness. They'd replaced Rose with Frances, so other than the constant ache of missing Rose, the clothing room wasn't much different. Frances's rheumatism exhausted her arms and legs by the time Manual Training began each afternoon, and Maxine made her lay out on a stack of towels while Maxine folded. She knew Frances hated that Maxine had to work harder because of her, so Maxine made sure to mention how much London was doing for Rose in Sick Ward. Frances understood.

Frances also didn't mind if Maxine rambled on about things like what it would be like to sail on a ship in the middle of the ocean, to be floating on water as deep as the sky was high. Frances said it took her mind her off her aching knees.

But today Maxine was quiet. She folded dress after dress without saying a word, while Frances lay on the towels.

"What are you thinking about?" Frances asked.

"Stealing money."

Frances laughed. "Really?"

"Yes."

"What would you do with it?"

"I don't know. Maybe buy Rose a bucket of Bit-O-Honeys. You know how she loves those things."

Frances laughed again. And then she lay quietly for a moment, before whispering, "I know where you can steal a lot of money."

Maxine stopped folding, the dress suspended in front of her.

London closed the book. She had once again finished chapter fifteen, Rose's favorite, where the hero, Dantès, imprisoned wrongly, digs a hole through his jail cell wall and finally, after years alone in a cold cell on an island in the middle of the sea, makes a friend.

It looked as though Rose were sleeping. But within a second of London's voice stopping, Rose's eyes popped open and she grinned.

"Fooled you."

"Did not. You're a shitty little liar. I knew you were awake."

"I like the abbé," Rose said. "I wish he didn't have to die."

"But he saves Dantès and gives him a great new life."

Rose frowned.

"You should sleep," London said.

"I'm not tired. I want to get up. Please, London."

"You can't. The doctor said your heart needs more rest."

"I don't care about my heart."

"Listen," London said, remembering Rose's stick. "I have a surprise for you."

"Maxine? Is Maxine coming?"

Crap. Now London had done it. "No, Rose, not Maxine, but something nice." London pulled the stick out from under the bed where she'd hidden it earlier because Rose had been asleep.

The girl beamed, clasping her hands together in silent happiness. She knew not to make a loud fuss.

"Damn, Rose," London snapped, handing her the branch. "You'd think I'd brought you a ham dinner." But London didn't feel snappish. Especially when Rose slid the stick beneath her blanket, closed her eyes, and released a happy sigh.

But then her eyes popped open.

"Do they let you visit Maxine and Alice, too?" she asked. "Like they let you visit me?"

London was disappointed the branch hadn't wiped out thoughts of Maxine. At least for a little while. She hated that she'd lied to Rose, pretending to visit her each day instead of admitting that the old woman had left her, and that she had no one. She'd tell the truth soon. When Rose's heart was better.

"Yes, I see Maxine and Alice," she snapped. Because now she felt snappish.

London thought about Maxine and her jelly bean of a plan, and then how Alice kept blinking at her, like somehow London could stop it all.

"Do you sit on the couches?" Rose asked. "The soft-looking red ones in the visiting room? Maxine always wanted to sit there."

"Sleep now, Rose," London said. "I'll be back later."

Rose closed her eyes and hugged her stick. Taking advantage of what was most likely momentary obedience, London hurried off to the crib room—away from couches and plans and missing sisters. It was dark and comfortable in the crib room, and she picked up Miriam and rocked her.

She loved the soft weight of the babies in her arms, even if they did reek worse than the scummy sewage bubbling in the harbor channel. She often read to them about the Count of Monte Cristo just as she did for Rose. Once they were bathed and changed and fed, she'd wander the dark aisles between the cribs reading about the island in the middle of a shark-infested sea, with its looming prison that no one had ever escaped. Except Dantès.

Gladys would linger nearby, looking for work that kept her close to the story.

"So, he climbs into the dead man's shroud, and sews himself inside?" Gladys asked.

"After dragging his friend's dead body to his own cell through the hole they'd carved in the wall."

"And he's thrown into the sea?"

"It's how he escapes," London explained. "Then he finds his friend's buried treasure and avenges himself on all his enemies."

Gladys thought Dantès went too far. London thought he might have gone farther, maybe killed that bitch Mercedes too, the girl who'd left him to die in prison. The only opinion the little yappers had was that London keep reading. Sometimes, after she'd been reading for half an hour and was stopping for a drink of water, the babies would begin to whimper and call out. The sound made Gladys laugh.

"They sure do like that story," she'd say.

London knew why. It was the same reason why she liked it. It was the only one they had.

January faded into February, and February moved into March, and the routine inside the crib room became comfortingly familiar to London. Nurses and doctors came and went, and other attendants now and then, but mostly the crib room belonged to Gladys, London, and the babies.

London visited Rose every day at the beginning and end of her shift, and always reported how Rose was doing to Maxine and Alice. The weekends dragged, as classroom time and Manual Training were replaced with choir and orchestra and Sunday school. All of which London despised. She chose to attend choir instead of orchestra because the music teacher let

London sit in a pew and re-wind the metronome when necessary, which wasn't often, and that made London's job very relaxing.

Weekends were made harder by Maxine's constant talk of the plan. Eloping.

It was impossible.

Maxine didn't see it. Alice did, but because she loved Maxine, she'd never say so. London didn't say so either, which was strange for her because she wasn't against the crushing of hope, if the hope was ridiculous, which this was. *Ridiculous.* There was no way the four of them were escaping. They might as well be locked inside the prison on Dantès's island, surrounded by the raging sea.

Maxine's plan had them stealing enough money to rent a flat and eat. But London couldn't think past the ten or so long, dark miles between Boston and Rose.

Rose.

She didn't seem to be getting better. Another thing London didn't say. London figured she didn't understand the heart, and so maybe it took longer than other body parts to heal. She hoped. Even if that hope was ridiculous.

On the Friday before Easter—the one they called "good"—the institution was whirring with visitors. London finished washing Miriam, who was sleepier than usual. The baby barely opened her eyes when London wiped her down with a warm cloth. Gladys was busy resupplying the medicine cabinet, and London was almost halfway through the weekly bathing when a doctor walked in followed by three visitors.

London knew the man to be an ass, and immediately moved toward Miriam, but he got there first, stopping next to her crib with a man and two women dressed in outside clothes and who were now holding handkerchiefs to their noses.

"Yes, the stench," said the doctor, and he smiled congenially. "It has been firmly established that the feebleminded emit a disagreeable odor."

London quickly sniffed her armpits and looked over at Gladys, who vehemently shook her head.

The doctor droned on about indolence and deficiency, but the visitors were hardly listening, too busy gawking at the sight of the children in the cribs.

"Are they human?" asked the man.

"They have a human origin," the doctor said. "Although, children such as these are insensitive to hunger, cold, and pain."

He reached into Miriam's crib and pinched her. Hard.

London gripped the metal of the crib she stood by to keep herself from leaping at him and ripping out his throat. Gladys thrust her head deep inside the cabinet with the sheets and towels.

"You see how it doesn't cry out? I know this would be painful to myself or any other normal being. But it doesn't have the same sense of pain as you and I."

He moved with the visitors through the aisles,

while they gasped at one baby and then the next. As soon as they'd moved far enough away from Miriam, London went to her, plucked her from her crib, and held her tightly against her chest.

The visitors huddled close together as they were guided through the room, stopping to stare into each crib while the doctor rattled off a list of diseases, disorders, and sicknesses afflicting the tiny humans lying in their beds. As they came closer to Gladys in her cabinet, the doctor stopped and smiled at her.

"Hello there, dear," he said. "How are you today?"

The visitors, unsure of themselves in this environment, and only feeling safe when standing behind the doctor, did not greet Gladys.

"Hello, doctor," Gladys replied. "I'm well. And you?"

The doctor turned to the visitors. "You see. Imbeciles are capable of affection toward those who treat them kindly."

He moved his party to the double doors, and the visitors, having seen enough of the dark crib room, quickly backed themselves out as the doctor lectured on, his muffled voice continuing after the doors closed. London and Gladys didn't move until they could no longer hear him.

"Prick!" London whispered, not wanting to alarm Miriam, still in her arms.

"Ignore it," Gladys said. "We have work to do."

"I didn't know you were an imbecile. I thought you were an attendant," London said.

"I am an attendant."

London couldn't help it, she laughed.

Gladys just shrugged.

Drawing Miriam away from her, London leaned to put the baby into her crib, but then stopped. The baby's head jerked, her eyes were rolled up toward her forehead, and her tiny legs and arms were twitching rhythmically.

"Gladys?"

The woman rushed over and inspected the baby, then stood back, not daring to look at London.

"What's happening?" London asked. "What's the matter with her?"

"She's having a seizure," Gladys said.

"How do we stop it? How do we make it stop?"

Gladys shook her head.

London grasped the infant closer as if to keep her away from Gladys's helplessness.

"London," Gladys said. "London, it's her time."

London shook her head, though she knew it was true. The babies were here to die. Were expected to die. Miriam was here because she was never getting better. Just as Rose was never getting better.

Rose was never getting better.

London felt as if she were spinning. As if she were turning round and round in a place without light, without air.

"We need to be here for her," Gladys said. "It's all we can do."

London held on to the seizing child. "The world is a shitty, shitty place," she cooed into the baby's ear. "I don't blame you for leaving it."

The seizure stopped, and London, relieved, looked up at Gladys and then back at the baby. But the relief was short, and Miriam entered a second seizure.

"Jesus," London said. "How long will this go on?"

Gladys said nothing.

Miriam stiffened in London's arms, the seizure stretching her out like a board. Her beautiful dark eyes disappeared into her eyelids, and her breath was short and raspy.

"Does it hurt her?" London asked

Again Gladys didn't speak.

"Does it fucking hurt her?"

"Yes," Gladys said. "I think it does."

The truth, as disgusting as it was, soothed London, and she held on to Miriam, never taking her eyes from the child's face. In that moment she thought of her mother, dying in a room in East Boston. Alone, except for a four-year-old who couldn't help or understand. But London remembered it now. The room. Her mother. The damp smell of illness. How she'd shoved her face against her mother's warm neck, sucked in the warmth of her, begged her to get up. Begged her to stop crying. But it had been London who'd been crying. The neck turning cold. And she'd been hungry.

"It won't be much longer," Gladys whispered.

It wasn't. Miriam took her last faint breath within the minute . . . and was gone.

The two of them stood together in the darkened room surrounded by the soft coos and clucks of the living. Holding on to the moment. Marking it for themselves. Marking it for her. Making it matter. The end of Miriam's short life.

After a while the sounds of the Sick Ward across the hall began to intrude. Coughing. The clanking of bedpans. A loud attendant giving someone the what for.

"We need to follow the protocol for a death," Gladys said. "You haven't done this yet. Would you like me to take care of Miriam, and I can teach you with the next . . . one?"

"No. Teach me."

London needed to do something, and if it wasn't some knobheaded protocol, it might be breaking a goddamn door from its hinge.

Gladys showed London how to fill out the yellow paper with the time when Miriam died and her number, and where they would file the paper when they were finished. They washed Miriam, and wrapped her in a clean sheet, and carried her down the hall to a locked door next to the locked door that led out of the Sick Ward. Gladys had a key. London had Miriam in her arms, her tiny body still soft and warm in the sheet. London did not think of her beautiful face, or the way she'd clicked her tongue whenever London had picked her up.

Gladys unlocked the door but didn't open it. "This is a hard place."

"Open it."

Gladys sighed, but she let London enter.

It was another large room with windows lining the far wall, like the crib room, but instead of being filled with cribs, it was crowded with tables covered in strange objects. In the dark, it looked almost haunted, and when Gladys turned on the electric lights, London saw that it was. She held Miriam closer as they entered.

It was a lab, or an operating room. Maybe both. Gladys let London take in the room. The smell burned her nose and tasted almost sweet. The tables were loaded with wires, lights, tubing, and a jumble of scales and small machines. But it was the jars that caught London's eye. Shelf after shelf of jars. With objects floating. And labeled with numbers like the ones they'd just written on Miriam's yellow sheet.

"Yes," Gladys said.

"Why?" London asked. "When they say we are incurable. Why would they cut us up? Are we that horrible that locking us away isn't enough?"

"Maybe to find a way to prevent it," Gladys said.

"We don't need to be prevented." She wanted to smash the jars. To pluck each one from the shelf and whip it at the floorboards with all her might.

Gladys stepped between the jars and London. "It's time to say goodbye."

"I said goodbye. She isn't here anymore."

But London didn't believe it. Not really. She thought about running. Clutching Miriam in her arms and getting her the fuck out of there. But to where?

It was over. There was no place to run, and worse, no reason to. She allowed Gladys to take the dead child from her arms, the emptiness causing London to wobble. She reached out to steady herself, but then pulled her hand back from the table. She didn't want to touch anything in this place.

Gladys took Miriam to a bank of steel iceboxes against the far wall of the room. After opening one and seeing it was full, she tried another. This one was empty.

As London watched Gladys slide Miriam into the chest, the girl in the iron lung sprang into her mind. It had been such a long time since London had thought of her. That machine, pushing the air in, pulling it back out. It had been months. Five months since the machine had taken over the girl's breath. Was she still alive? London hoped she was. London had always hoped the girl would live. She hoped a lot of things, she realized, watching Gladys close the chest door.

"Icebox number twenty-six. We write that down next to the time of death." And Gladys did. "Now we file the paper where I showed you, back in the crib room."

London followed her out without looking back.

The claps sounded a half hour later as London sat by Rose's side. The girl was sound asleep, looking smaller than she'd ever looked, her stick tucked against her chest.

The world is going to hell in a handbasket.

God, London missed the old lady. Of course she'd been right. She had always been right. The world *was* going to hell in a handbasket.

And London felt the pull of it.

Alice stuffed a third deviled egg into her mouth, the tangy cream of this one tasting just as delicious as the first. Deviled eggs. They had them once a year, on Easter. Alice loved deviled eggs. She swallowed the third, gulped down milk, and picked up her fourth. All while trying not to look at Maxine, who was staring down at her untouched breakfast.

"What's the matter with her?" London asked, though she knew the answer, and also that Alice probably wouldn't respond.

"What if I forget the song right in the middle of it?"

"The song only has one word," London said.

"I'm playing it. Not singing it."

"Well, we can all thank our lucky berries for that," London said, "because I'd rather scratch my ass pimples than listen to you sing. But your piano-playing rates."

Maxine smiled. "Thanks."

Alice watched the girls as she ate another egg. Her

stomach was beginning to hurt now, which meant she only had another egg or two left before she'd have to stop.

"I'm glad you'll be with Rose," Maxine said. "Can you really hear the service from the Sick Ward?"

"Gladys says we bundle everyone up, and then open all the windows. She says that the talking parts are hard to hear, but the music is like it's playing right on a phonograph in the room with you. Especially the organ. She says you can hear the organ best of all."

Again Maxine smiled. "It's like she'll be with me."

"You should eat," Alice said. Maxine had lost a lot of weight while Rose had been sick.

"You want my eggs?" Maxine asked.

"I'll take 'em," said London.

Maxine shoved them across the table toward London. Alice sighed.

Looking forward to Easter had kept Maxine going. Alice was dreading what came next. The *beach*. Always the *beach*. But the beach was a bunch of applesauce. It didn't matter how much money they saved. Four of them running off? They'd be caught quicker than the pantry cats catch kits in short grass. Not that it mattered. Because they were going nowhere without Rose, and Alice knew that Rose was going nowhere. She could see it in London's eyes. Rose was sicker than London was letting on.

Alice stuffed in her last egg. It was harder to swallow when she worried, yet she choked down the creamy yoke while she watched London eat Maxine's.

Easter.

They had five more months until they graduated to the adult dormitory. Five more months to figure out what Alice hadn't been able to figure out in almost five years. London would go. As soon as Rose was well. London would run. And she wouldn't take the three of them with her.

She watched London beg an egg off Edwina, who waved her away. Just because the girl didn't speak didn't mean she didn't eat. Edwina turned fifteen this spring. And following the May Day dance, to which all the fourteen-year-old girls were invited, she would move up. Neddie, twelve going on thirteen, had another two years. She'd be assigned another high-grade moron to watch over her. Neddie and Edwina had been together for three years. Alice noticed that Edwina passed her egg to Neddie under the table. Neddie giggled as she shoved it into her mouth.

London rolled her eyes. "Fuck you two," she said, but it wasn't said meanly. London was one of the only people Alice knew who could curse and make you feel warm inside.

She was changing, London. Accepting this place. Or maybe she was starting to like them all. Or at least she liked Manual Training. Monday couldn't come fast enough for that girl. Taking care of Rose and the babies. Although, she rarely spoke about the babies. That was how much she liked them. At Fernald, you kept your trap shut about the things you cared most about. For some reason that Alice did not understand, once what you loved was let loose into the world, it was as if the machine that churned the institution day in and day out—the people, the files, the testing, the routines—conspired to take it away. You needed to hide the things you loved. Like Rose's stick in the heating grate. Loving was dangerous. It made you weak. It made Alice weak. It made Maxine weak. It was making London weak.

Four claps.

Maxine leaped from the table, knocking over her empty milk glass.

"Shit," London grumbled. "It's just a song."

Maxine's mouth twitched, but she didn't respond. And she didn't remind London not to cuss. Alice watched Maxine a little more closely then, and saw that it wasn't the song. There was something else on Maxine's mind, something else she was nervous about. And the five, or six, or maybe seven eggs Alice had eaten rolled in her stomach.

After lining up, they marched out of the dining hall and toward the chapel. The school was crawling with people. Like at Christmas, the community was invited to the chapel to join the institution's Easter celebration. It was the last day of March, but winter clung. The grass was wet with slightly frozen dew, and the cold air blew from their mouths like smoke. As much as Alice hated the clapping, the circles, the excusing, the day-to-day never-changing routine of this place, there was also a comfort in it, a comfort she didn't feel now, trudging through the slushy dew behind Maxine, wondering what it was that was going on. And why she hadn't seen it before.

Out of the corner of her eye, she saw London break off the line and head toward the North Building. Alice almost reached out . . . wanting to grab her back.

London.

Alice had come to depend on that girl, especially in moments like this, when Maxine was about to do something that could get her in trouble. Alice never wanted to tamp down Maxine's happiness or excitement. There wasn't enough of it, and when it cropped up, it was so golden, so bright, like an afternoon hour on the benches by the window with the winter sun shining down on your head. But whatever it was that Maxine was up to had to be stopped, and London never had any problems shutting down golden things. Although, all Alice could do was watch London's long dark braid swing into the distance.

Alice stood up straighter, looking around for Ragno. The large white woman was huffing beside Frances, the girl's arm clutched in the attendant's grasp, Ragno dragging Frances along to keep pace with the group. Alice shivered. She knew how much Frances hated to be touched like that.

They were only a hundred feet from the entrance to the chapel. Alice leaned in. "You'll do great today," she whispered. If she got Maxine talking, maybe she could stop what was happening. Maybe even find out that nothing was happening.

But Maxine didn't say a word. Instead she did something she never did, not unless they were lying on their cots in the dark. She swung her hand back toward Alice and grabbed the tips of Alice's fingers, squeezing them.

Alice panicked.

"What are you doing? Maxxie? What's going on? Tell me."

Maxine wouldn't turn around.

"Don't do it," Alice said. "Don't. Whatever it is. Please."

Alice immediately tried to suck her words back in. They were too loud, too filled with pain, with fear. Alice's bad foot turned in, and she stumbled.

"You need to walk, girl," Ragno snapped from behind her.

They were allowed to feel—the attendants, the nurses, the doctors. To snap in anger at you for not walking fast enough. To shiver with cold during circles, needing to take turns with other attendants while the girls walked on. To become emotionally attached . . . to their children, their husbands, their wives. All of it somehow marking them as normal. But for Alice to cry out in pain because of her aching foot, to reach out and touch Maxine's warm hand, to scream in anger at not being able to stop this next horrible thing from happening—all of it marked her a degenerate.

Maxine now broke off the line, heading toward the back door to the chapel. Alice could see Miss Petruskavich give her a wave. She could see the bright smile on the music teacher's face. Just like Alice couldn't stop London from walking away, she couldn't stop Maxine. Off Maxine went, and all Alice could do was keep walking while she stared after her.

Alice entered the chapel, filed into the pew, and took a seat between Helen and Mary.

"You smell like eggs," Mary complained.

Alice ignored her. She was sure she did smell like eggs.

The service began with a hymn sung by the women's choir. Alice didn't bother looking for Maxine, who was tucked away wherever the organ was. The music stopped, and the minister climbed to the pulpit and spoke. Alice usually enjoyed the sound of his voice as he lectured, the deep tone of his rising and falling pleas to God creating a sort of calm that she looked forward to. But today his voice irritated her.

She felt a chill, and breaking her eyes away from the minister, found Ellen staring at her.

Alice was careful not to change her expression, not to twitch one single muscle as she once again focused on the minister. Ellen was always watching now. Alice knew she wasn't Ellen's ultimate target—that was London—but this didn't mean Alice was safe, or Maxine. Because Alice and Maxine, they were London's stick. And Ellen knew it.

The minister lectured on, talking about the rolling away of rocks and the rebirth and new life. Alice's stomach began to cramp. Sweat gathered on her forehead. She wanted to hear those hallelujahs. Needed to hear them. Once they rang out, Alice somehow felt sure that whatever Maxine was planning to do, it would be over, and maybe Rose would get better, and maybe summer would come, and maybe it would all work out.

The sermon finally ended, and the men's choir sang two hymns, long ones with so many verses that Alice couldn't tell if this was still Easter Sunday, or possibly they'd been here an entire week already. Helen bumped her arm, looking sideways at her. Alice straightened up.

One of the men from the choir stood and sang alone as people passed golden plates back and forth through the pews to collect offerings. The girls in her row didn't look up in anticipation because a plate would not pass their way. None of the plates were ever passed through the inmates.

Alice had never experienced time moving so slowly. The man sang on and on. The golden plates passed from left to right, and then right to left, the money piling higher and higher.

At last the song ended. The congregation stood. Alice stood with it. But her stomach seemed not to follow, at least not right away. She swayed, gripping the pew in front of her.

The organ struck a strident note, and now everyone sang, "Praise God from whom all blessings flow," and the golden plates were carried in triumph up the center aisle to the lectern, spilling over with . . . clams!

Alice's stomach flipped, taking all the eggs along for the ride. The whine that emerged could not have been louder. Helen tsk-ed her, and Mary moved away. There were a few giggles from the crowd. A second whine followed. Now Alice would have done anything for a little music, but the church was silent.

The third time her stomach called out, Ragno's red face caught Alice's eye. The attendant motioned angrily for the girl to leave the pew. Permission given, Alice stumbled over a hundred feet in her haste to leave the chapel. She had been periodically excused for so many years that she didn't recognize at first just how close she was coming to releasing however many deviled eggs now furiously wanted the heck out of her stomach. People watched behind smiles of embarrassment. But her life had been full of watchers, and this sweaty moment of distress felt no different.

Making it out of the double doors of the chapel, she clomped down the steps to the Sunday school rooms, where she knew there were toilets. She prayed, for the very first time inside this building, that the doors would not be locked.

They weren't.

Alice listened to the Hallelujah Chorus from her toilet seat. It was one of the strangest moments of her life. Listening to Maxine play and a church full of people singing, while taking a shit all by herself for the first time that she could remember.

"Maxine," she whispered, "don't steal it all, baby. Just don't steal it all."

London couldn't believe it. Maxine had stolen thirty dollars from the collection plate. That was a lot of kale! The molly didn't just beat her gums. She followed through, even if her plan was still way off the tracks. Not only was it Monday, London's favorite day of the week, but they now had stolen more money than London had ever seen at once. Although, she hadn't quite seen it, since Alice had snatched it straight from Maxine and most likely already had it buried in their borax box.

Alice. That girl could be as jumpy as a damn street cat. She rated at both the mangles and with a needle, two skills that London saw could pull favors in this joint. The girl might have lived it rich in here if she hadn't fallen in with the wrong crowd. The thought of Maxine and Rose being the wrong crowd made London laugh . . . which made Wally gurgle up at her.

"It slays you too, right?" she said to the baby in her arms.

"Put that child down and get to work."

Gladys wasn't serious, and London didn't listen to her. At least not for another minute or two. But then London swaddled Wally and picked up Doris. Monday was always a busy day since the weekend attendants couldn't be counted on to do much, and all the infants needed to be bathed, changed, and fed. London only had time to pop in to say good morning to Rose and make sure the girl was feeling better after yesterday.

Easter had been one gloomy flat tire in the Sick Ward. Maybe the doctors—sitting their healthy fat asses in their cushioned church pews next to their wives and children—had envisioned the degenerates of the Sick Ward bundled into clean white blankets and lined up smiling in front of the large opened windows of the North Building while they listened to the beautiful voices of the choir, accompanied by the thunderous organ ringing out across the great lawns of the institution. Though this was exactly how London had described it to Maxine and Alice the night before, the reality had been very different. The reality had been a room packed with a bunch of sad sick clunkers brought even lower by a holiday spent freezing in front of an open window with no family, no ham dinner, and no day of celebration.

Rose had held it together until Maxine's first chord. Then her sore, aching heart had broken apart.

Who knew that the babies in their dark, quiet crib room would be better off than the people in the wards across the hall from them, with the sun streaming in and a spring breeze wafting over them?

Today was a Monday and nothing more, and London was thrilled by it.

She finished feeding all twenty-six babies in the crib room, and then went to read to Rose.

They were in the final chapters of the book once again. London had lost count of how many times she'd read it. Rose didn't mind the end, where the two young lovers are reunited, but she didn't like all the revenge that took place before it.

"Why do the mother and son both drink the poison?"

"They just do," London said, going back to reading.

"I wouldn't drink the poison."

"Of course you wouldn't, Rose. You're not a murderer like Madame de Villafort."

"Can you read it where the boy doesn't drink it?"

London read on, leaving Edward de Villafort out of the death. *Why not?* she thought. It gave her a thrill to keep him alive. Also, it made Rose happy.

Although, a few chapters later, Rose insisted that Danglars, the most evil man in the book, be given a chicken to eat while he was in prison.

"No, Rose. Danglars is a prick. I'm not giving him a chicken."

"He's starving, London."

"It's a story, Rose."

"But he's starving in the story."

"Sorry, Rose. Even for you, I refuse to give that bastard a chicken."

Rose scowled, but she let London read on, at least for a little while before stopping her again, this time to have her skip where Maximilian drinks the poison.

"Come on, Rose. You know Maximilian doesn't even die, and that the count is going to give him everything he ever wanted."

"Don't you think it's wrong that the count makes him think he's dying?"

"It didn't bother you last time I read it."

"It did bother me. I just didn't say anything."

"Do you want me to stop reading?"

The woman in the bed next to Rose's spoke up. "You girls do know there are other books, right? Other stories you could read?"

Rose and London looked at each other, and London—her back to the woman—rolled her eyes. Rose grinned. It was the first time that Rose had smiled since Easter morning.

"Thanks, Mildred," Rose said. "But this is the book we read."

They heard the woman sigh, and London shrugged her off and got back to the story. This time Rose let her read straight to the end, where the people that the count didn't kill or make kill themselves all find love and money and happiness together.

"*Darling*," London read, "*has not the count just told us that all human wisdom is summed up in two words? 'Wait' and 'hope.'*"

London closed the book with a smack. "It's a shit ending," she said.

"Maybe he shouldn't have killed everyone," Rose said, as she always did. "Then the ending could be different. The count is like a rotten egg, I think."

"Remember he was locked up for a long time, Rose. And no one gave a crumb about him."

"Mercedes cared. Her heart was broken."

"Not so broken that she couldn't pick up in a week and move on," London snapped. "People are crap, Rose."

"Just like the old lady says," Rose whispered.

London shut up then. She'd never told Rose that the old lady had left her. And that London lived here now. Just like Rose did.

"Do you think she still says that kind of stuff, London?"

London should have known that Rose knew, but what came as a real surprise to her was that London was happy Rose knew . . . happy to share things that had once felt necessary to keep tucked into the dark, cramped places of herself.

"Yes," London said. "I'm sure that old woman is somewhere hanging out a window and yelling horrible shit at people."

"Probably in Chicopee," Rose said.

"What?" asked London.

"Probably she's in Chicopee," Rose repeated. "That place she likes."

London stood up. Rose was right. London could hear that shrill raspy voice as plain as day. "Chicopee!

Did you hear me! Chicopee, goddamn it!" That's where she was! The old lady hadn't walked out on her. Hadn't left her. Thelma Dumas was out there waiting for her in the only place in the world where bad shit didn't happen. Chicopee, Massachusetts.

Why hadn't London seen it before? And the money. They had the money. Maybe, just maybe, Maxine's plan could work. And Rose could get better. Why couldn't she? She absolutely could.

"You're smiling," Rose said.

"Am I?" London asked, touching her face.

"You almost never smile."

"Don't I?"

"No, you don't."

Maxine could smell the spring air even though she and Frances were locked in the windowless clothing room. It was the first of May, or May Day, and a big dance was planned for the women of the institution. On the list of those invited were all the girls on the cusp of fifteen. It would be their first chance to mingle with the girls from the women's dormitory, since they'd be heading there come fall. Or rather, *some* of them would be heading there. Others would not.

They were eloping. The four of them. Soon. Maxine was sure her plan would be a success now that London was in on it. Folding dress after dress, she dreamed of the house by the sea . . . even if London had told her Chicopee was inland. There'd be a river for sure, or a lake or pond. She didn't need the smell of salt—the ripples on the water would be enough. Moving water, Alice's hand in hers, and Rose.

Rose.

The only wrinkle Maxine could see in the plan was Rose getting better in time. And of course, she would. They had four months before September. Four months of warm weather in which to find the exact right moment to run. London had explained that it would take them approximately two weeks to walk west to Chicopee, between Alice's foot and Rose's weak heart. London had already figured out the route with the help of the woman she worked with in the Sick Ward. London said the woman would never give them away, and Maxine believed her. She believed everything London told her. London was in charge . . . but it had been Maxine who had stolen the money.

Well, she and Frances. Although, Frances only wanted the five dollars she'd promised Bessie, so that Bessie and Ellen would leave her alone. The rest she let Maxine have. For Bit-O-Honeys. For Rose.

Maxine didn't even feel guilty for lying to Frances. This was how she knew she was ready to leave and why she knew the plan would work. She was willing to steal, to lie. London said that lying and stealing were sometimes necessary. She said the school was lying to them, and that none of them deserved to be locked away. London didn't know about the alley, though. Always that alley. But if London said they didn't deserve to be locked away, they didn't.

They would leave Fernald, all together, and live forever with London's mean old lady. Maxine couldn't wait. And as if all this weren't enough, tonight they would dance. She smiled at the dress she was folding. Now that they were leaving, the bad things at Fernald didn't seem so bad and the good things seemed even better.

There was a shuffling outside the clothing room door, and Maxine quickly woke Frances. The key turned in the lock, and Miss Sweeney stood in the doorway.

A dance *and* Miss Sweeney on duty. Maxine's smile grew even larger.

"Well, aren't you the chirpy one," Miss Sweeney said.

They walked the circles in the misty rain, ate dinner, and instead of an hour in the day room before periodic excusing, the girls who would be attending the dance were marched upstairs to tidy up some, which meant standing in the bathroom and washing their hands and faces, and maybe brushing their hair. There were six of them old enough to attend the dance— Edwina, Alice, London, Bessie, Ellen, and herself.

Maxine's smile never dimmed—not in the rain, not when dinner turned out to be burned pea soup left over from lunch, and not when the six girls were locked in the bathroom for more than an hour. At least not at first. But then the hour lingered, and Maxine looked around the room and remembered Christmas Eve, standing at this very sink, Ellen sitting on her toilet just as she was now, the horrible scene that had come next.

Then . . . as if life really were a lovely dream, the key clicked in the lock. Maxine had never heard a more beautiful sound. And they were on their way to an actual dance.

The group was led out the front doors and across the institution's grounds toward the gymnasium, where the dance would be held. Maxine had never had this view before. Walking across the institution's lawn under the setting sun. The rain had stopped. The trees were greener than she'd ever remembered them. Even the air smelled exciting, like it had been cracked wide open and she could spread her arms out as far as they could reach and never touch the edges of it.

London smacked her from behind, and Maxine dropped her arms.

When they finally entered the gymnasium, Maxine stumbled as she took in its transformation. The walls were covered in paper flowers. Streamers hung from window to window in great sloping curves. Tables, piled high with tiny cakes, lined the entire right side of the room. And Miss Pet, her hair done up in a high bun, sat, poised and ready at the far end of the gymnasium behind a phonograph. Maxine clasped her hands together to contain her joy and looked over at Alice, who returned her excited gaze. The dance was already more than Maxine had ever imagined it could be, and the music hadn't even started.

They were made to stay in their line until name

badges could be affixed to their dresses. As the girls waited for Miss Sweeney to tag them, more and more women poured into the gymnasium, until Maxine could no longer see the windows or the door.

A scratchy sound collected the crowd together in a single gasp, and then the first song rang out—followed by a burst of applause. Maxine had never heard music like this, in a room full of chatting, laughing people, and if any of the others had, obviously not often enough that the occasion didn't warrant the extra cheer.

Miss Sweeney, who was now pinning on Maxine's name tag, had to ask Maxine to stop jumping or else she'd be poked straight through with the long pin. Maxine tried, but it was nearly impossible, and she did get a poke or two before her name could be secured to her dress. But she barely felt it. She couldn't feel anything. *This is happiness,* she thought, *where you can be poked with a pin and not feel a thing.*

The dancing started, and Maxine stood transfixed, watching the darting arms and legs, the bobbing heads, the bodies twisting and spinning. Touching was allowed today, as everyone dancing had to touch, and again Maxine looked for Alice. She discovered Alice standing across the room, eyes focused on the dance floor just as Maxine's had been, her mouth open in wonder. Maxine stared at Alice, a new sensation making her heart beat more strongly—or maybe it was Alice's mouth.

Maxine backed herself away from the dance floor in order to keep watching Alice, the room growing darker as the sun sank beneath the treetops. All of a sudden lights popped on all around them, hundreds and hundreds of tiny lights strung like it was Christmas.

This was the best night of Maxine's life.

The scratch of the phonograph caught her attention, and she ran to Miss Petruskavich, and because touching was allowed tonight, she threw her arms around her teacher.

"Maxine!" the woman cried. "How delightful."

"It is delightful!"

"Have you danced yet?"

Maxine became shy. She hadn't. Although, she wanted to. So very much.

Miss Pet read her fear. "There's no wrong way to dance," she told the girl. "Think how you sway sometimes when you're playing the piano, when the music climbs inside and you can feel the notes moving you. That's dancing. Go out there and listen to the music. And then do whatever motion the notes tell you to do."

Maxine still wouldn't leave her teacher's side, so Miss Pet tried another way.

"I'll play a special song for you. It's called 'Ain't She Sweet.' Now go out there and dance."

Maxine obeyed. The way she'd been trained, when she was told to do something, she did it.

Standing on the dance floor, she did what Miss Pet had said and closed her eyes and listened. It worked just the way she'd said it would. First a tickle in her stomach. Then a wobble in her shoulders. Another moment had her hips swaying and her chin bobbing. It was her feet that took the longest to come around, being the most timid of her body parts and not able to find a natural way of moving. She finally opened her eyes and watched the women dancing around her, and picking up on their stepping motions, she gave it a try.

Dancing full on now, she looked up for her teacher, who gave an approving nod.

Maxine danced every song . . . though she was sweating quite a lot and her throat was dry and she'd do anything for a quick drink of water. Anything but leave the dance floor. Once, in a truly twisty song, she swung around and saw London sitting in a chair eating cake. Maxine called out to her, "Come dance!"

London glared back, stuffing cake into her mouth, white icing squeezing out the sides of her lips. Maxine laughed. She couldn't even imagine London dancing. Or Alice.

Alice. In all of Maxine's dancing, she had lost track of Alice. She now searched the room and found her doing exactly what London had been doing, stuffing her mouth full of cake. For the first time since Miss Pet had sent her out onto the floor, Maxine stepped outside the beat of the music. Maybe she should be eating cake too? She lamented that these events had been scheduled simultaneously.

Alice's eyes met hers. Maxine grinned and waved.

"Come dance," she yelled. To her great surprise, Alice put down her cake and stood up.

Maxine's stomach fluttered as Alice made her way past the elbows and knees of jigging women, until she stood in front of Maxine.

"Hi," Maxine said, in a high-pitched voice she never used. Alice blinked at her, and Maxine was sure that Alice noticed her strangeness.

"I've never done this," Alice admitted.

Alice's confession soothed Maxine. "I never had either. But you just wiggle," she said. "Like this." She laughed at herself as she shook her butt and swung her arms up in the air. To her absolute joy, Alice imitated her.

Grinning, Maxine shimmied. Alice shimmied. Maxine swung her arms right. Alice swung hers right. But then Alice did a twirl, all the way around in a circle on her good foot so that she ended up looking right back into Maxine's eyes. Maxine responded with her own twirl. And the dancing continued. First Alice leading, and then Maxine. If Alice's foot hurt or got in her way, she sure wasn't showing it. Song after song, the girls danced. Sweating and breathing heavily and staring into each other's eyes. But then Alice reached out . . . took hold of Maxine's hand.

Touching was allowed. But was what Maxine felt allowed? She stopped looking into Alice's eyes then, and it seemed like her own sight turned inward and all she could see was spinning color.

Alice twisted Maxine under her arm, and flung her out across the dance floor until their arms, outstretched, pulled taut. Maxine looked at her then. Alice. Attached to her, happy. Alice was happy.

"Look!" Alice cried, gesturing to the stepping and turning the other women were doing around them. Not letting go of Maxine, Alice began to imitate the others, stepping forward, side, together, and then forward, side, together. Maxine studied them quickly and joined in.

Now they were connected by both their hands, dancing with each other across the wooden gymnasium floor, taking cues from the other dancers, twisting each other in and out and under. Always with their feet, forward-side-together, back-side-together. In this way, they taught themselves to fox-trot, though they didn't know its name, and then to tango, a funny dance where they held tightly to each other and did strange kicks while swinging one another about in jerky motions. Miss Pet kept the music going, and Maxine's stomach hurt with the happy combination of dancing and breathing.

At one point Alice screamed over the music, "I'm so thirsty."

"Me too!" Maxine said, and laughed. Neither had any intention of leaving the dance floor. Leaving each other. Touching was allowed. And Maxine clung tightly to Alice's sweaty hands, slammed awkwardly into her soft body, sucked in her hot breath, reveled in the movement of Alice's neck, her chest, her legs. As if Miss Pet could feel Maxine's heart about to explode, she slid the last song off, and Maxine found herself panting, looking into Alice's eyes.

"We're going to slow things down for a song or two before the May Day speeches begin," Miss Pet called out across the gymnasium.

All around them they heard groaning. Every institutional event required listening to long-winded speeches, mandating a massive amount of clapping. But Alice and Maxine didn't groan. They didn't move. They stood there, on the dance floor, holding hands.

There came a crackly moment of silence before the needle met the vinyl. A moment that Maxine was so sure how to fill that the words she spoke weren't words at all, but just the next thing meant to happen in the world.

"I love you."

She did. Love Alice. Never more than in this moment, with Alice's beautiful eyes so close and her sweet breath flowing toward Maxine's mouth, and Alice's chest rising and falling and rising and falling. Except, it had stopped. Alice's chest.

Maxine dropped her eyes to the gymnasium floor. The music began, slow and whiny, but Maxine's shoulders didn't move. Or her feet. She felt as though the sweat was running off her like that river she so hoped ran through Chicopee, and she wished she could close her eyes and make this moment disappear, but if her eyes closed, she didn't trust herself not to spin to the ground.

Then she felt Alice's hand. On her back, pulling her close. And fingers, sliding in between her fingers, with Alice's chest, rising and falling again, against her chest, and her own lips, brushing up against Alice's braid. The music softly wailed around them as the girls swayed, their breathing slowly coming together, so that when Alice breathed in, Maxine breathed out, and when Maxine breathed in, Alice, out, bringing their bodies closely together.

Maxine's head spun with the sweet smell of Alice's sweat mixed with the sharp smell of cake icing. Except for with Rose, Maxine had never been this close to another body. But Rose's body was Maxine's own. Alice's body was not Maxine's. At all. In fact, Maxine could feel every part of it that wasn't hers, the skin of Alice's neck against her chin, Alice's breast pressing in below Maxine's own, the touch of Alice's hand against her back. She'd never felt this kind of warmth. Like it was coming from inside her. Had Alice understood her? Maxine ached for her to have understood.

As much as she didn't want to, she pulled back from Alice, not stepping away, but enough to face her, their bodies continuing to sway to the music.

"Alice," she said. "Rose and I are here, at Fernald, because of me. When I was ten years old and playing in the alley beside my house, I kissed Evelyn Heminger. My mother caught me. She said I wasn't normal. And that she didn't want me around my brothers. Rose and I . . . It's my fault."

She'd gone this far. And Alice was still holding on to her. Holding on to her more tightly. Maxine could feel it. So she said it. "Evelyn wasn't the only girl I kissed. I belong here."

It was then that Maxine noticed the square white teeth in Alice's mouth. Because she was smiling.

"Maxxie" was all Alice said, before she leaned in . . . and kissed her.

London leaped from her chair, but didn't dare move toward them, not yet anyway. Better not draw attention to the two girls on the dance floor *making the fuck out!* She couldn't believe it. Did they not understand what they were doing?

Frenzied, London scanned the room. Women were dancing, eating, talking, laughing—no one seemed to notice Maxine and Alice. London was just about to take a seat, wait until the song was over to rush the dance floor and plant those two. But then they pulled apart, and London let out the breath she'd been holding . . . until, across the room, between the now separated lips of Alice and Maxine, London saw Ellen. Smiling directly at her.

London's heart dropped, and out of it tumbled all the hope she'd been feeling since she'd discovered that the old lady hadn't left her and that Maxine had stolen the Easter offering. In its place was dread, a hard, tight dread.

It took all of London's strength to smile back at Ellen, the most wicked smile she could muster. But she couldn't keep it up, and she stuffed the last of the cake into her mouth, and swallowed it whole in a dry lump that almost refused to slide down her throat. Ellen disappeared into the crowd, and London didn't waste a second. She was out on the dance floor, her fingers clutching Maxine's skinny wrist and yanking her toward the back door, where London had seen the women leave from, to smoke.

"Ouch," Maxine called. "London, you're hurting me."

London checked behind her to be sure Alice was following. She was.

Once outside the door, she let go of Maxine and approached the first woman she saw smoking. "Bum a gasper?"

The woman stared down at London, deciding whether or not she'd give her a cigarette.

"Oh, give her one, Rita. The kid's one of 'em coming up," said a woman smoking in the group.

Rita begrudgingly slid one from her deck.

"Match?" London asked.

She could feel Maxine and Alice standing behind her, wondering what was happening, yet too out of their element to say or do anything.

Rita reached into her pocket, pulled out a pack of matches, and slapped them onto London's open palm.

"Thanks," London said, turning and motioning for Alice and Maxine to follow her around the corner of the gymnasium into the dark. No sooner had they turned the corner than London flipped the cigarette into the grass and sprang on the girls.

"You're leaving, tonight. Now."

Alice stared, and Maxine's mouth opened and then closed. She was too stunned for words.

"Ellen. She saw the kiss."

Now the girls reacted, stepping away from London and looking around, like Ellen might be behind them, or worse, Ragno.

"Listen to me—" London began.

"But Rose—" cried Maxine.

"Listen to me," London repeated, stepping close to Maxine. "They will separate you. Forever. Do you understand? It's tonight or it's never."

Maxine squirmed under her gaze like a trapped animal.

"Ladies," a voice called from the door.

The girls froze.

"Ladies, it's speech time. Please come inside."

They heard grumbling, but the group of smokers at the back door herded inside, and the door closed, leaving the three of them in darkness. London waited one moment and then spoke. "The borax box."

Alice nodded. "Maxine," she said.

Maxine's face was already wet with tears, but she also nodded.

Alice leading, the three of them streaked across the institution's lawn to the back of the laundry building.

Alice arrived at the tree first and started to toss the rocks aside.

"I can't go. Rose. I can't go," Maxine babbled.

"You have to."

"London."

London turned to Maxine then, grabbing her by the shoulders. "You have no choice. Do you hear me, Maxine? You have to go. I'll take care of Rose. You know I will. I will never leave her. Do you understand? *Never*." She was heaving, breathless, stung by the truth of what she was saying.

Maxine's face glowed back in the dark. She understood.

Alice had the borax box out of the wall and was emptying the money from it. She pulled off her boot, and then one leg of her stockings, shoved the change and bills into the foot, and then replaced her stockings and boot. This surprisingly smart act inspired London.

"Follow me. Bring that box."

London scoured the lawn for movement. It was well past eight, and no one was about. Any maintenance staff would be hanging around the gymnasium, smoking with the women and hoping for leftover cake. They ran around the back of the large North Building that housed the Sick Ward. The only other building in sight was the nurse's home, which was a good two to three hundred feet away, with trees between the girls and the home.

London yanked Maxine and Alice to the large-leafed

tree nearest the laboratory's window, one floor above them.

Maxine was seriously struggling to hold herself together. Alice looked grim. London, who was about to climb a tree, smash a window, and start a fire, was feeling very much herself.

She addressed Alice. "Chicopee is north of Springfield."

Alice dropped her face to the dark grass.

"Alice," London snapped. "It's time to stop wondering if this piece of shit place has you pegged right. You won't make it out of here if you believe these pricks. Neither of you will. Now," she barked. "Repeat this. Left on Trapelo, left on Lexington, right on Boston Post Road, all the way to Springfield."

"Left on Trapelo," Alice whispered. "Left on Lexington. Right on Boston Post Road all the way to Springfield."

"Chicopee is north of Springfield. Find Springfield, and you'll find Chicopee."

"The old woman?" Alice asked.

London hesitated, but only for a moment. "She'll be there. I know it. Just . . . walk around the town. Look for an open window with an old lady cussing out of it. That will be her. Thelma Dumas."

"Dumas," Alice said. "Like your book."

"Like my book." London smiled. "Now, Trapelo is that way, at the edge of the school." She pointed to her left. Tell me again."

"Left on Trapelo. Left on Lexington. Right on Boston Post Road to Springfield," Alice repeated.

London glanced over at Maxine, who was still breathing heavily, but was quiet.

"Travel only at night. Sleep during the day. Steal only what you have to." London turned and looked up at the window of the laboratory. "Wait here. I'm going to throw some stuff down." She took the borax box from Alice and stuffed it under her dress.

Sucking in one last breath before she started to climb, she thought about telling them that she wasn't coming back down. But her instincts told her to climb, so she climbed.

It was easy. One floor. London loved scaling walls or trees, loved being high above the ground. Once she reached the window, she peered inside. No one. She pulled the borax box from under her dress, stuck her hand inside, and then smashed the window, all uncertainty gone.

"Watch out," she whispered as she pulled shards of glass out of her way, and let them fall to the grass below. After slipping her hand inside to unlock the window, she opened it and crawled in without so much as a scratch.

"Stay there," she called down.

She raced to the door of the lab, unlocked it, and eased it open. Again, no one. Out in the hall she entered the quiet crib room. She knew no one would be in here at night; the attendants stayed away from the room if they could.

"Hello, you dirty little fleas," she whispered to the babies, maneuvering between their cribs to the supply cabinet. After grabbing a waterproof sheet, she threw in a bunch of tins of the awful milk-like food, along with a tin opener. Then she grabbed two clean blankets, knowing the girls couldn't carry much more than this. At least they wouldn't starve or freeze in the first few days.

She ran back for the door and checked the hallway once again. She could hear coughing and shuffling coming from the ward across the hall but saw no one. She made her move, racing back into the lab, closing the door silently behind her, and then running for the window.

They were watching.

She hung the tins wrapped in the blankets out of the window without dropping them, waiting for Alice and Maxine to move out of the way. Then she let them go. The blankets hit the ground with a clank.

Alice immediately picked them up and began shoving the two blankets under her dress and rerolling the tins back up in the plastic sheet. Then she tossed the sheet over her shoulder.

"Go!" London called.

The girls stood under the window . . . not moving.

"Go!" she repeated, pointing toward Trapelo Road.

They slowly turned from her and began to walk, and then to run. She watched them until they got to the corner of the North Building, two dark spots now.

Then one of them stopped and turned. It was Alice.

She raised her hand in the air . . . and waved.

London raised hers.

They'd make it. She knew. Alice would do this. She'd get them there.

And then they were gone.

London didn't waste any more time. She ran to the long shelves of jars with the numbers on them. She couldn't make out any of the numbers in the dark, and she was glad for it. After grabbing the largest she could find, she moved back to the broken window, as far from the Sick Ward and the crib room as she could get. She placed the jar on the floor, picked up the nearest heavy object she could find—a thick glass container—and smashed the jar. The liquid flooded the floor, the smell burning London's nose. She lit a match. And dropped it.

The fire whooshed into existence faster even than London had expected it to. Now with a little light, she looked around the room for more fire power.

After collecting three more smaller jars in her arms, she carried them to the flames and set them far enough apart to give her time to move away.

Smoke began filling the room.

Rushing to the door, London's plan was to open it and cry "Fire" as loudly as she could. Get the hysteria moving, and then hide until she could safely join the throng of people exiting, which was sure to follow. But as she approached the door, the first jar exploded, throwing her against the door. The fire leaped higher, heading up the wall toward the ceiling. London crouched by the door, her arms over her head, coughing. Behind her, the two other jars exploded like gunfire.

The smoke was so thick now that she could barely see. She heard someone outside the door. "Fire!" a woman screamed. "Fire! Fire! Fire!"

London swung open the door, the fire leaping at her from behind. She stumbled out into the hall and slammed the door, her hands burning from the heat of the metal knob.

Smoke billowed from under the door so that she couldn't see her boots. She was going to kill everyone. Already the door to the Sick Ward was unlocked and people were scrambling past her to get out. Panicked, she ran down the hall toward the Sick Ward. She could hear fire bells in the distance. Passing the rush of bodies leaving the ward, she fought her way toward Rose.

She found Rose in her bed. Anyone who was mobile was already up and moving toward the exits. Someone had opened the large windows, and a few people were standing on the sills. The room wasn't smoky yet, or hot. They still had time.

"Rose," London said, but she was already throwing back the blanket, and had the girl in her arms.

"My stick," Rose cried. "My stick, my stick!"

London stopped, letting Rose reach down. If London was going to kill them both, the least she could do was let the girl die with her lousy tree branch. All London had wanted was a diversion. Something to distract from Maxine and Alice's escape. Not this. Not this.

London stumbled toward the doors, struggling to stay on her feet and not drop Rose, or trip over the stampede of people ahead of her.

The hallway was now full of smoke and people. They could no longer get past the laboratory door. There was confusion and screaming, and London was sure she and Rose would be trampled. Many were returning to the Sick Ward, back toward the windows. The drop to the ground was only twenty feet or so, enough to break your legs maybe, but not kill you. Unless you were very sick, and then just maybe? London couldn't stop to think about what she'd done, putting all these people's lives in danger. The babies' lives in danger.

The babies!

London shoved her way across the hall and through the double doors of the crib room. Kicked the doors closed behind her in an attempt to keep out the smoke. There wasn't any smoke in here . . . yet. She carried Rose to the farthest corner of the room and set her down on the floor under a window.

"Don't move."

"London?" she asked.

"Everything's fine," London snapped. And Rose smiled.

London unlocked the window and threw it open. Sticking her head out, she had to cover her ears with her hands, the roar of the fire was so loud. There was a crowd forming below to the right. To her left the flames were shooting out of the lab windows.

London pulled her head back in. Smoke was curling under the double doors, and the room was heating up.

"Rose," she said, and grabbed a handful of towels from the supply cabinet and threw them down at the girl. "Rose, I'm going for the babies."

London ran to the far side of the crib room and grabbed Louie. She was shaking too hard to pick up Edwin, too. She ran back and placed Louie in Rose's arm.

"Oh," Rose breathed. "What's his name?"

But London was gone. For Edwin, and then Wally, and Doris, and William, and Shirley . . . running from crib to Rose and back again, over and over, laying each of the babies gently down around Rose, until every crib was empty.

Sweat dripping down her face, her eyes burning with smoke, London held Lois in her arms, the last child from the cribs.

"Look at all your babies," Rose said, coughing.

Smoke. Too much smoke.

London stared at all the children surrounding Rose. They were her babies, and so she had better goddamn save them.

Stepping over the pile of infants, Lois still in her arms, she stuck her head out the window. "Over here," she shouted, her voice cracking from the smoke. She waved her one arm. "Help! Help!" But they couldn't hear her over the blast of the fire.

The smoke was thickening. The heat was intense. London didn't know what to do. She searched the room for something, anything.

She handed Lois to Rose and ran to the supply cupboards, grabbed an armful of towels, and ran to the double doors. She tried desperately to stuff them into the cracks to hold back the smoke. It was useless.

Forced to her hands and knees by the coughing, she crawled back to the window. Her eyes were burning. Fire trucks had driven right up onto the lawn, and men were uncoiling hoses. "Help us!" she screamed, knowing there was no way anyone could hear her. Sucking in a breath to scream again, she could only break down into a fit of coughing.

"Rose," London gasped over the deafening hiss of the fire. "They can't hear me."

"Throw my stick," Rose screamed.

London grabbed it from Rose's hands. She moved to the window, picked the nearest crowd of people she could see through the smoke, and whipped Rose's stick at them.

It hit. And within a minute a group of people on the ground were looking up at London, shouting at her, shouting at others, collecting under the window.

London picked up Lois. Hung her out the window. Knowing she had no choice, she watched the men and women below, huddling together, arms raised. And then she . . . let the baby go.

They caught her!

Now London grabbed Edwin, checked to see that the people below were ready, and dropped him. One after another through the relentless coughing, the sweat pouring off her, and her lungs and eyes burning, she dropped baby after baby to the waiting crowd, not thinking, really, how they were going to catch Rose. Or her.

When she grabbed the last baby, Ruth, she whispered down at Rose, "You're next."

But when she turned back to the window, a sweaty face greeted her. A man, with his arms out. On a ladder. London handed him Ruth. And he was gone.

The smoke was so thick now that London had to hold her sleeve over her mouth to breathe. She knelt on the floor and picked up Rose. When she turned back, the man was at the window again, and she heaved Rose into his arms. But Rose clutched at London's dress and wouldn't let go.

"I'm right behind you."

Rose let go. And London didn't wait to see her reach the ground but scrambled over the window ledge onto the ladder as soon as the man had begun to descend.

Her feet never touched the ground. She was snatched from the ladder rungs. London fought them off, shoving and kicking, but she was exhausted, and couldn't stop coughing, and soon collapsed into their arms.

She could feel the cool air of the night and hear the roar of the flames traveling farther and farther away from her, or she from them. She was on her back, on some sort of stretcher. It stopped. Someone wiped the sweat from her face with a wet towel, and then poured water into her mouth. It scorched her throat, and made her choke, but she wanted more and more, clutching at the hands that held the pitcher to keep it to her mouth. After sucking in a lake full, she dropped her head and breathed in deeply for the first time since the fire had started.

"Rose!"

She grabbed at the person holding the pitcher. "Please, where is she?"

But now she was moving again. Across the lawn. She tried to sit, but hands pushed her down.

Up, up, up she went, toward electric lights. She knew the steps. The columns. The door. She was back at the dormitory. Home. Once inside, they turned right, into a room London had never been in before . . . the visiting room.

They placed the stretcher on the floor, and when London turned toward the couch, there Rose was. Sitting among the soft cushions. Grinning.

"I love you, London."

London's mouth jerked. Only one person had ever told her they loved her. Alby. That night. When he'd whispered it into her ear after the second time they'd done it. London had wondered if it were true, if he did love her. She'd been confused, and hadn't known what to say back to him, so she'd said nothing.

"I love you too, Rose."

Alice held Maxine's hand, fearing Maxine might turn at any moment and bolt back to the institution. The first explosion happened as they reached Trapelo Road. Alice squeezed Maxine's hand but kept them moving. The second and third blasts that followed only served to speed them up. It was dark, but even so, Alice didn't trust the road, and the girls stumbled along a few feet inside the tree line, crunching through leaves and stumbling over rocks hidden beneath.

About a mile out, Maxine couldn't keep going, and yanked Alice to a stop. They stood panting in the woods, watching the flames lighting up the night sky. The fire sounded like the loudest rainstorm Alice had ever heard.

"Rose," Maxine whispered.

Just her name. But Alice understood it was Maxine's heart breaking. And she stood close, knowing it was all she could do.

After a few minutes of shivering, Alice realized she had to move them.

"It was a summer day," she said, still watching the flames over the tops of the trees. "My brother, he said, 'Come on, Alice.' That's it. Just, 'Come on,' but I figured it was bad. I figured whatever happened next was going to change everything. He bought me candy. Bit-O-Honey, the ones Rose loves. I ate it because he'd paid for it. But I don't remember tasting it. I was too scared for tasting things."

The girls turned from the fire.

"Are you scared now?" Maxine asked.

Alice thought for a minute. Was she scared?

"No," she said. "Not scared. Sad. Sad it isn't just like you dreamed it."

They began to walk away, from London and Rose and the institution. The leaves rustled under their feet and the fire roared at their backs, its intensity lessening in their ears with every step.

"Where were your mother and father?"

"My mother died when I was born. My father died of sickness when I was four or five. I remember him, though. He talked a lot. Ate a lot. Laughed a lot. My father was not a quiet man."

"You're like your mother, then," Maxine said.

"Hm," Alice said. "Maybe. Maybe I am."

Alice talked them straight through the first three nights, the stories bobbing up like apples floating in a barrel. It was as if being released from the institution released the memories of everything that had come before, and as each memory bobbed to the surface, she'd tell it to Maxine, slowly, to match the pace of their stride.

Hungry all the time. Thirsty all the time. They buried tin after tin of milk until there were none left. Alice stole them eggs from a henhouse on the sixth night, which they ate raw.

Maxine cried herself through the long days hiding in the woods. For Rose.

Instead of worrying about the soft nut and the hard shell, Alice cried too. For Rose, for London, for Mary and Edwina and all of them. And also, for herself. For the little girl whose life had been a series of events directed by others, so much so that waking in the woods, she fully expected a whistle to blow over their heads from the tree branches. But what came next was up to her now. And she'd rouse Maxine, roll up their things, and climb back up onto her aching foot. She had been wrong. Loving didn't make you weak. It made you strong.

When they finally entered Springfield on the morning of the tenth day, they used their first bit of money to buy a loaf of bread for nine cents and ate the whole thing before asking which way it was to Chicopee.

It was a three-mile hike north. They decided to walk through the day, and arrived before noon.

The town was bigger than the girls had imagined, and they wandered up and down its streets for two days with their chins in the air, looking for that open window, before they heard someone shouting from one street over. They quickly followed the sound and came upon two thin forearms jutting over a sill, a gray head of hair cropped short, and deep frown lines creasing a woman's face.

Alice and Maxine clutched hands.

"Thelma Dumas?" Maxine called up to the window.

"What the hell do you two grubby little loo loos want?"

Maxine looked at Alice and smiled.

They'd found her.

EPILOGUE

Thelma Dumas let the two filthy, exhausted girls in. She fixed her room for them, told them she slept in the chair every night. The white one believed her. The black one didn't.

Since she was no liar, she slept in the chair every night, and it became true.

They said London would soon follow. When no one was watching, she'd leap out a window with another girl named Rose, and they would make their way here. Again, the white one believed this, and again, the black one did not.

Neither did the old woman.

She remembered the day the agency had dropped London off. Angry and dirty. Often when the orphanage had a wild one, they'd dump the girl on the old lady. She never minded the wild ones. Thelma knew that kind of wild. The kind the world didn't have any use for—girls who bit and scratched at life. And somehow they all seemed to disappear. Like her girl had.

These two weren't wild, but Thelma kept them. Just as London had known she would. Six months later, in October of 1929, the stock market crashed and everything went to shit, exactly as the old lady had always said it would. But all the better for them. Everyone was kept busy scraping for a bit of bread, and not out searching for two missing degenerates.

HISTORICAL NOTE

The early twentieth century saw the emergence of a powerful union between science and social policy, called eugenics—the pseudoscience of human improvement through human breeding. The initial idea of eugenics was to use the budding science of heredity to eradicate human disease and vice. What it quickly became was a social system that rounded up the usual historical suspects—the poor, the disabled, and the marginalized (including people of color, indigenous people, immigrants, and members of the LGBTQIA+ community)—and institutionalized them for life.

During the 1800s, educators in the United States began schools for children with disabilities. These institutions were founded with good intentions. However, by 1900 the country was beginning to change. Industrialization, immigration, urbanization, labor unrest, capitalism, racial tension, and changes in social morality all gave rise to great uncertainty. The paranoia generated by these factors was directed into the creation of a category of people to scapegoat for society's ills: the feebleminded—children and adults who might reproduce their "kind."

To rid the gene pool of "unworthy" human traits, and thereby "unworthy" humans, there began a collection of people with physical, mental, intellectual, and moral differences, through massive standardized intelligence testing, the court system, the culling of orphanage populations, and the finger-pointing of neighbors. The United States gathered its "others," segregating them into institutions. All of this was done in the name of human betterment using the "science" of eugenics.

As if segregation were not enough, a campaign of sterilization followed. A policy begun in 1907 in Indiana and confirmed by the 1927 Supreme Court ruling in *Buck v. Bell* stated that any man or woman deemed unworthy to procreate by any doctor could legally be sterilized against the person's will. It is estimated that seventy thousand people were compulsorily sterilized between 1907 and 1980.

Eugenics in the United States took the idea of human betterment and defined "better" as middle- to upper-class white, straight, able-bodied men, along with middle- to upper-class white, straight, able-bodied women who conformed to the social and moral standards of the day. Anyone who fell outside these boundaries was in danger of being institutionalized and/or sterilized.

The United States was not alone in its eugenics programs. From Latin America to Europe to Asia, the eugenics movement flourished. Adolf Hitler, using the "science" of eugenics and its ideas on "better" humans, murdered six million people deemed to not be "better" humans.

The word "eugenics" may have been relegated to the trash bin of history; however, the movement's ideas are still alive and well. What makes a better human? An able body, an intellectual mind, the color of one's skin, the sex one is assigned at birth, conforming to a certain gender or to the idea that sexuality is binary, falling in love with the societally accepted gender, the possession of neurotypical functioning, the contents of one's bank account, the numbers in one's zip code? In the United States all of these criteria have been used, and are still being used, to determine who matters and who doesn't.

The Massachusetts School for Idiotic and Feeble-Minded Youth (which later became known as the Massachusetts School for the Feeble-Minded, and then the Walter E. Fernald School after the death of Dr. Walter Fernald) began in 1848, and continued well past the time of London, Rose, Alice, and Maxine, not closing its doors until 2014. The structure, patterns, and routines of this institution, along with many others like it across the United States, would change little in these 166 years. The world would go on . . . forgetting about the people inside these institutions. Unfortunately, today we are still undoing the damage created by the idea that diversity should be punished rather than celebrated.

AUTHOR'S NOTE

All of the discriminatory statements made by doctors and nurses in this novel were actually written by doctors and nurses in real life. I lifted their exact words and phrases from documents and reports, changed pronouns or verb tenses as needed, and dropped the statements into the story whole. Today we are astounded by ideas like Dr. Fernald's about Maxine's criminality being biological, and diagnoses using words such as "idiot," "imbecile," and "moron" would be ridiculous. It can be easy to look back at the past and wonder how anyone believed such absurd things. A much harder task is to look around ourselves right now and wonder what words and ideas we absolutely believe to be true that will later turn out to be ridiculous.

All my life I've played a what-if game—relocating myself to other moments in history. *What if* I had been born in a hunter-gatherer society? As a woman, I'd have been a gatherer. This always makes me happy because I think I would have made a good one. I love being outside, and I'm great at finding things. *What if* I had been born during the Great Depression in the United States? Like so many other readers of John Steinbeck's *The Grapes of Wrath*, I wonder if I could have been as strong as Rose of Sharon in the shocking but strangely hopeful ending of that novel. (No spoilers here. You have to read it.) I began writing *The Degenerates* by playing this very game. *What if* I had been born during the height of the eugenics movement in the United States? As someone born with a spinal disorder causing extreme body difference, I might have been institutionalized for life along with Alice, Maxine, Rose, and London.

In playing this game, I am understanding history by understanding my place in it—the privileges I garner from being born white, the disadvantages of being born in a disabled female body, and so on. Playing it brings me closer to understanding others. As humans, there are so many experiences that we share. But there are also so many experiences that we don't. Understanding these differences with an empathetic heart and an open mind is truly the beginning to understanding not just history but what it means to be a better human.

Finally, just as I lifted the words of doctors and nurses from documents to use in this novel, I also lifted my characters from those same documents. Where only the notes of medical professionals and researchers remain, I attempted to see the people. London and Alice and Maxine and Rose (and all the other characters that populate this novel) may be fictional, but many people lived the lives found in these pages. In an effort to respect difference and disability, I've attempted to give the diagnoses of each character where it's possible.

London—London was pregnant. She was also unmarried, which gave her a diagnosis of being morally feebleminded.

Maxine—Maxine most likely would have identified as homosexual, because in 1928 this would have been her only choice in vocabulary. In modern medical history, homosexuality was considered a medical diagnosis and could be found in the Diagnostic and Statistical Manual of Mental Disorders. The medical community viewed homosexuality as a sign of a defect. This diagnosis was not removed from the manual as a mental disorder until 1973.

Alice—Alice most likely would have identified as homosexual (for the same reasons Maxine would have). Alice was also born with congenital talipes equinovarus (often called clubfoot). The affected foot appears rotated internally at the ankle. It has a variety of causes, although we don't know what caused Alice's talipes equinovarus. Today talipes equinovarus can be corrected by placing the foot into multiple casts over the course of several weeks, or by surgery.

Rose—Rose was born with Down syndrome. Down syndrome occurs when an individual has a full or partial extra copy of chromosome number twenty-one. (Most individuals have forty-six chromosomes; in Down syndrome, there are usually forty-seven.) This full or partial extra copy of a chromosome causes physical growth delays, mild to moderate intellectual disability, and characteristic facial features. In the novel, Rose is referred to as a Mongoloid. This reference was brought into use by Dr. John Langdon Haydon Down, a nineteenth-century physician. (The syndrome is also named for him.) While working with the self-advocate population (a contemporary name chosen by people with intellectual and/or developmental disabilities to represent themselves—it signifies having a voice of one's own), Dr. Down came to the (very wrong) conclusion that these individuals had regressed to an earlier state of humanity that he (once again, very wrongly) believed was the state of being Mongolian. He eventually abandoned these beliefs, yet the term continued for more than a century.

Lizzie—Lizzie was born with hydrocephalus, the state in which someone has excess amounts of cerebrospinal fluid (the liquid that surrounds and protects the brain), resulting in pressure on the brain. This can lead to an enlarged head, slowing of mental capacity, cognitive deterioration, headaches, vomiting, blurred vision, difficulty in walking, and drowsiness. Today we can often help people born with hydrocephalus with a medical device called a ventriculoperitoneal shunt.

Frances—At some time in Frances's life, she contracted rheumatic fever. Rheumatic fever is an inflammatory disease that can develop as a complication of strep throat or scarlet fever. It causes painful and tender joints—most often in the knees, ankles, elbows, and wrists. It can also cause uncontrollable body movements and outbursts of unusual behavior. Rheumatic fever still exists, although it is more common in underdeveloped countries, and linked to poverty.

Sarah—Sarah might have been diagnosed today with autism spectrum disorder. Autism spectrum disorder (ASD) is a developmental disorder that impacts a person's communication and behavior. While doctors and scientists do not know the exact causes of ASD, research has suggested that genes may act together with influences from the environment to affect development in ways that lead to ASD.

Neddie—Like Rose, Neddie was born with Down syndrome.

Edwina—Edwina had mutism, which could have occurred for several different reasons. Elective mutism is when psychological issues, including trauma, cause a person to not speak. Selective mutism is when a person wants to speak but in certain circumstances finds that they cannot (often caused by anxiety). Total mutism is when a person doesn't speak under any circumstance. Physical damage to the brain or speech muscles can also cause mutism.

Miriam—Miriam was born with an unknown

congenital malformation, as well as perhaps hydrocephalus (which may have led to her seizures). "Congenital malformation" is another word for "birth defect." Birth defects can be caused by genetic or environmental factors, or a combination of the two. In many cases, doctors and scientists do not know the cause.

Louie, Edwin, Wally, Doris, William, Shirley, and Lois (and all the other babies in the Sick Ward)—Unfortunately, there were (and are) many causes of infant mortality. There could have been any number of medical reasons why the babies were placed in this room, with some babies undoubtedly having more than one condition.

Characters in the novel that are not in this list—There were many characters who lived in the institution who are not listed here with their diagnoses. They symbolize all the children and adults who were segregated from their families, friends, and communities for nothing more than being different.

BIBLIOGRAPHY

Anderson, V. V. *State Institutions for the Feeble-Minded.* New York: National Committee for Mental Hygiene, 1920. archive.org/stream/stateinstitution00ande#mode/2up.

Baker, L. W. *Mental Epilepsy.* Reprint from *Medico-Legal Journal*, December 1886. Howe Library Historical Pamphlets on Disability Studies, circa 1810s-1960s, Robert D. Farber University Archives & Special Collections Department, Brandeis University. http://bir.brandeis.edu/handle/10192/27330.

Blatt, Burton, and Fred Kaplan. *Christmas in Purgatory: A Photographic Essay on Mental Retardation.* Boston: Allyn and Bacon, 1966.

Carlson, Elof Axel. *The Unfit: A History of a Bad Idea.* Cold Spring Harbor, NY: Cold Spring Harbor Laboratory Press, 2001.

Clark, A. Campbell, C. M'Ivor Campbell, A. R. Turnbull, and A. R. Urquhart. *Handbook for the Instruction of Attendants on the Insane.* Boston: Damrell & Upham, 1893. archive.org/stream/handbookforinstr00clar#page/n3/mode/2up.

Cohen, Adam. *Imbeciles: The Supreme Court, American Eugenics, and the Sterilization of Carrie Buck.* New York: Penguin Books, 2017.

Comfort, Nathaniel C. *The Science of Human Perfection: How Genes Became the Heart of American Medicine.* New Haven, CT: Yale University Press, 2012.

D'Antonio, Michael. *The State Boys Rebellion.* New York: Simon & Schuster, 2005.

Davis, Angela Y. *Women, Race & Class.* New York: Vintage Books, 1983.

Davis, Lennard J. *Enforcing Normalcy: Disability, Deafness, and the Body.* New York: Verso, 1995.

Dilts, Andrew. "Incurable Blackness: Criminal Disenfranchisement, Mental Disability, and the White Citizen." *Disability Studies Quarterly* 32, no. 3 (2012). https://doi.org/10.18061/dsq.v32i3.3268.

Doll, Edgar A. *Clinical Studies in Feeble-Mindedness.* Boston: Richard G. Badger, 1917. archive.org/details/clinicalstudiesi00doll.

Dolmage, Jay Timothy. *Disabled upon Arrival: Eugenics, Immigration, and the Construction of Race and Disability.* Columbus, OH: The Ohio State University Press, 2018.

Engelman, Peter. *A History of the Birth Control Movement in America.* Santa Barbara, CA: Praeger, 2011.

Ferguson, Phil. *Infusing Disability Studies into the General Curriculum.* National Institute for Urban School Improvement. impactofspecialneeds.weebly.com/uploads/3/4/1/9/3419723/urbanschoolsdisabilities.pdf.

Fernald, Walter E. *Some of the Methods Employed in the Care and Training of Feeble-Minded Children of the Lower Grades.* Faribault, MN: Press of the Faribault Democrat, 1894. bir.brandeis.edu/bitstream/handle/10192/27536/309%20p-14.pdf.

Fitch, William Edward, ed. *Pediatrics: A Monthly Journal Devoted to the Study of Disease in Infants and Children,* Vol. 25. New York: Pediatric Publishing Company, 1913. https://hdl.handle.net/2027/nnc2.ark:/13960/t4gn0ts20.

Goffman, Erving. *Asylums: Essays on the Social Situation of Mental Patients and Other Inmates.* Chicago: Aldine, 1962.

Harper, Peter S. *A Short History of Medical Genetics.* New York: Oxford University Press, 2008.

Hollander, Bernard. *The First Signs of Insanity: Their Prevention and Treatment.* London: Stanley Paul & Co., 1912. archive.org/details/firstsignsofinsa1912holl/page/n5.

Kerlin, Isaac Newton. *The Mind Unveiled: A Brief History of Twenty-Two Imbecile Children*. Philadelphia: U. Hunt & Son, 1858. archive.org/details/mindunveiledorbr00kerl/page/n7.

Kevles, Daniel J. *In the Name of Eugenics: Genetics and the Uses of Human Heredity*. New York: Knopf, 1965.

Kline, Wendy. *Building a Better Race: Gender, Sexuality, and Eugenics from the Turn of the Century to the Baby Boom*. Berkeley, CA: University of California Press, 2005.

Leonard, Thomas C. *Illiberal Reformers: Race, Eugenics, and American Economics in the Progressive Era*. Princeton, NJ: Princeton University Press, 2016.

Linton, Simi. *Claiming Disability: Knowledge and Identity*. New York: New York University Press, 1998.

Lippmann, Walter. "Tests of Hereditary Intelligence." *The New Republic*, November 22, 1922. www.disabilitymuseum.org/dhm/lib/detail.html?id=1727.

Lombardo, Paul A. *A Century of Eugenics in America: From the Indiana Experiment to the Human Genome Era*. Bloomington, IN: Indiana University Press, 2011.

Lombardo, Paul A. *Three Generations, No Imbeciles: Eugenics, the Supreme Court, and* Buck v. Bell. Baltimore: Johns Hopkins University Press, 2008.

Macdowall, Margaret. *Simple Beginnings in the Training of Mentally Defective Children*. London: Local Government Press Co., 1921. archive.org/details/simplebeginnings00macd.

McCann, Carole Ruth. *Birth Control Politics in the United States, 1916–1945*. Ithaca, NY: Cornell University Press, 1999.

Mukherjee, Siddhartha. *The Gene: An Intimate History*. London: Vintage, 2017.

Myers, Caroline E., and Garry C. Myers. *Measuring Minds: An Examiner's Manual to Accompany the Myers Mental Measure*. New York: Newson & Company, 1921. archive.org/stream/measuringmindsex1921myer#mode/2up.

National Institute for Urban School Improvement. *On the Nexus of Race, Disability, and Overrepresentation: What Do We Know? Where Do We Go?* Tempe, AZ: Arizona State University,

December 2001. www.niusileadscape.org/docs/FINAL_
PRODUCTS/LearningCarousel/On_the_Nexus_of_Race_
Disability_and_Overrepresentation.pdf.

National Research Council Psychology Committee Subcommittee
on Methods of Examining Recruits. *Examiner's Guide
for Psychological Examining in the Army.* Washington, DC:
Government Printing Office, 1918. archive.org/details/
examinersguidefo00nati.

Onians, Edith C. *The Men of To-Morrow.* Melbourne, Victoria,
Australia: Thomas C. Lothian, 1914. archive.org/details/
menoftomorrow00onia/page/n7.

Ordover, Nancy. *American Eugenics: Race, Queer Anatomy, and the
Science of Nationalism.* Minneapolis: University of Minnesota
Press, 2003.

Pintner, Rudolf. "The Mental Indices of Siblings." *The Psychological
Review* 25, no. 3 (May 1918). bir.brandeis.edu/bitstream/
handle/10192/27453/624%20p-56.pdf.

Rosen, Christine. *Preaching Eugenics: Religious Leaders and the
American Eugenics Movement.* New York: Oxford University
Press, 2004.

Sherlock, E. B. *The Feeble-Minded: A Guide to Study and Practice.*
London: Macmillan and Co., Limited, 1911. archive.org/
stream/feeblemindedguid00sher#page/n5/mode/2up.

Spiro, Jonathan Peter. *Defending the Master Race: Conservation,
Eugenics, and the Legacy of Madison Grant.* Lebanon, NH:
University Press of Vermont, 2008.

State of New York, State Board of Charities, Department of
State and Alien Poor, Bureau of Analysis and Investigation.
Eleven Mental Tests Standardized. Albany, NY: Eugenics and
Social Welfare Bulletin No. 5, 1915. archive.org/stream/
elevenmentaltext00newy#mode/2up.

Stiker, Henri-Jacques. *A History of Disability.* Translated by William
Sayers. Ann Arbor, MI: University of Michigan Press, 2009.

Stuckey, Zosha. *A Rhetoric of Remnants: Idiots, Half-Wits, and Other
State-Sponsored Inventions.* Albany, NY: State University of
New York Press, 2015.

Terman, Lewis M. *Genius and Stupidity: A Study of Some of the Intellectual Processes of Seven "Bright" and Seven "Stupid" Boys.* Pedagogical Seminary, Vol. 13 (September 1906): 307–73. archive.org/details/geniusstupiditys00term.

Terman, Lewis M. *The Measurement of Intelligence: An Explanation of and a Complete Guide for the Use of the Stanford Revision and Extension of the Binet-Simon Intelligence Scale.* Cambridge, MA: The Riverside Press, Houghton Mifflin Company, 1916. archive.org/stream/measurementofint1916term#mode/2up.

Trent, James W. *Inventing the Feeble Mind: A History of Intellectual Disability in the United States.* New York: Oxford University Press, 2017.

Washington, Harriet A. *Medical Apartheid: The Dark History of Medical Experimentation on Black Americans from Colonial Times to the Present.* New York: Harlem Moon, 2006.

Winzer, Margaret A. *From Integration to Inclusion: A History of Special Education in the 20th Century.* Washington, DC: Gallaudet University Press, 2009.

ACKNOWLEDGMENTS

So much gratitude to Chloe Morse-Harding, reference and instruction archivist at the Robert D. Farber University Archives & Special Collections, Goldfarb Library, Brandeis University, for all your help within the Samuel Gridley Howe Library collection, and to Laurie Block, executive director of the Disability History Museum.

Society owes a great debt to historians, and I owe an extra-special debt to this incredible group of them: Dr. Zosha Stuckey, who specializes in teaching rhetoric, writing, and social justice at Towson University; Dr. James W. Trent of Brandeis University's Heller School for Social Policy and Management; Dr. Paul A. Lombardo, Regents' Professor and Bobby Lee Cook Professor of Law at the Georgia State University College of Law; and Peter Engelman, associate editor at the Margaret Sanger Papers Project.

Many, many thanks to the following people for their

excellent medical advice: Brian Skotko, MD, MPP, the Emma Campbell Endowed Chair on Down Syndrome and director of the Down Syndrome Program at Massachusetts General Hospital; Jeanhee Chung, MD, internist with Massachusetts General Hospital; and Juliana Hiraoka Catani, MD, attending physician at the Women's Unit, Samaritano Hospital.

All my love goes to those who read, including Sarah Cassell, Leslie Caulfield, Lisa Majewski, and Irene Vazquez.

Heaps of appreciation to Reka Simonsen, Julia McCarthy, Rebecca Syracuse, Clare McGlade, and Bara MacNeill—the most tenacious team in the industry.

And to Kerry Sparks—there's a lot of London in you (and I mean this in the best way possible).